D1176894

Oxygen

OXYGEN

ANNABEL LYON

The Porcupine's Quill

CANADIAN CATALOGUING IN PUBLICATION DATA

Lyon, Annabel, 1971–
Oxygen

ISBN 0-88984-212-4

1. Title.

PS8573.Y62099 2000   C813'.6   C00-930829-6
PR9199.3.L98099 2000

Published by The Porcupine's Quill,
68 Main Street, Erin, Ontario NOB 1TO.
Readied for the press by John Metcalf; copy edited by Doris Cowan.
Typeset in Trump, printed on Zephyr Antique laid,
and bound at The Porcupine's Quill Inc.

This is a work of fiction. Any resemblance of characters to persons,
living or dead, is purely coincidental.

Represented in Canada by the Literary Press Group.
Trade orders are available from General Distribution Services.

We acknowledge the support of the Ontario Arts Council,
and the Canada Council for the Arts for our publishing program.
The financial support of the Government of Canada
through the Book Publishing Industry Development Program
is also gratefully acknowledged.

1 2 3 4 • 02 01 00

Canada

for my family

CONTENTS

Black   9

Stars   21

Hounds   27

Watch Me   33

Things   43

Sexy Rex   51

Tea Drinks   55

Song   63

Joe in the Afterlife   71

Letters and Numbers   79

Run   85

Trials   97

Every Little Thing   101

Awake   109

Play   115

BLACK

The old woman upstairs is taking a long time to die. Downstairs, Jones is making some phone calls. Jones calls Barry and Edith, and Tom and Anna, and Jack and Ruby and Glen. He calls Denise. He calls Larry and Kate and Bridget and Amy. He calls Foster. He calls Suzy and Morris.

'God, Jones,' Morris says. 'I'm so sorry.'

'But will you come?' Jones asks.

Morris pulls on the phone cord, stretching Jones's voice out and letting it seize back to coils, a kid with bubblegum, finger to tongue. 'Do you really think,' Morris says. 'At this point, I mean.'

'Yes,' Jones says.

'I mean, considering.'

'Yes.'

'Will Lorelei be there?'

'Lorelei, Lorelei,' Jones says. 'Are you coming or not?'

'Is this really the right time?' Morris says.

'I want to see everything go up in the air and come down again different,' Jones says. 'I think this is the thing I've been waiting for.'

'This thing is your mother dying.'

'Morris,' Jones says. 'You have to at least think about it.'

'Suzy won't want to.'

'I think you should be here for this,' Jones says.

* * *

Suzy doesn't want to go.

'Come on, Suzy,' Morris says. 'Why are you being so difficult?'

'I just don't want to,' Suzy says.

'You'll regret it later in life.'

'No.'

'We're going and that's final.'

Morris is forty-three and Suzy is five.

* * *

9

There are complications. First, Suzy needs a dress.

'A dress!' Suzy shrieks, as though he has suggested a crucifixion or a gentle roasting. She runs around the house, flapping her arms. A dress!

Morris is dark but Suzy is blond. She has never worn a dress a day in her life.

'Come on, Suzy,' Morris says. 'It's not so bad.'

'Have you ever worn a dress?' she asks.

'Yes,' he says.

'How was it?'

'You get used to it,' Morris says. 'You have to get the right kind, that's all.'

'What's the right kind?'

Black satin bias-cut with skinny little straps and a velvet train. Did he really, all those years ago? 'Well, now,' Morris says. 'Let's see.'

* * *

Morris and Suzy take the bus downtown. He pays and she looks out the window.

Morris thinks about dresses and little girls in dresses. He thinks about sturdy cotton, blue and white stripes, dresses Suzy could fall down in and people would worry about her first. Morris loves Suzy and wants her to be pretty and happy. He knows this is a contradiction and it distresses him pleasantly, like love. It draws his love for her out ahead of him in a long ribbon, trailing him along, flustered and anxious and determined to get things right.

Suzy thinks about construction paper and glue. She thinks about spreading a thin pool of glue into her palm and letting it dry and peeling it off again and how it makes a print of her skin, and how her palm is cool and sticky-dry afterwards. She thinks about scissors and the heavy feel of cutting and the sound, like a lion's snarling purr. She thinks about looping noodles of white glue all over the world.

They find Suzy's dress on a hanger on a rack in a large department store. Morris knows it when he sees it. The dress is plain yellow with a green satin sash and a bow above the bum. He selects yellow running shoes to go with the dress. Suzy steps from the cubicle, pretty as May, and lets the saleslady zip her up. Morris is delighted.

'What do you say?' he says to the saleslady. 'I mean, what do you say?'

The saleslady looks at Suzy, who is kicking at herself in the mirror with the toe of her new running shoe.

'Thank you, Morris,' Suzy says.

* * *

Another complication: will Suzy have to kiss the corpse? It happens that way in films. Angelic white-blond child is led to the open casket; creamy blond woman splinters, twenty years on, into something unrecognizable. Sometimes she will wear black, sometimes white; sometimes she will smoke, sometimes not. Morris doesn't like to think of Suzy smoking, although he likes to think of the elegance of smoke in black and white.

He gives her a colour bath. Yellow hair, blue mat, orange towel, white hooded robe. A happy child's bath.

Morris sits on the toilet seat and watches Suzy play with her fish, a fat orange fish with yellow sunglasses. Inside its mouth sits a smaller blue fish with the pleasing form of a nut. Suzy pulls the blue fish out of the orange fish's mouth and lets them go in the water. The orange fish gobbles at the bathwater, eventually closing on the blue fish with a click.

Suzy has forty-seven bath toys – Morris has counted them. Today, she pulls the blue fish too hard and the ratchet jams, snapping the string. She pales, a fish in each fist.

'We'll find another one,' Morris says quickly, wondering where Lorelei procured such a hideous toy. He offers Suzy one of the neglected forty-six, a turtle. She tries to stuff the turtle into the orange fish's mouth.

Tonight, and every night after tonight, Suzy must sleep with the fish. The orange fish does not worry her so much any more, but the blue fish weighs upon her heart like a stone. She puts it in her mouth, gags, takes it out. She sleeps with it against her lips, hoping her breath will keep it warm.

The house of Jones and his mother has the feel of a party, a laid-back Sunday-afternoon extended family get-together with stocking feet and beer cans and sports on TV for those that want it, but hushed in deference to the woman dying upstairs. It feels like a house full of people who just happen not to be in any of the rooms Morris wanders into. It hums, it buzzes, it breathes. Morris is surprised that Jones, being Jones, has achieved such a thing.

Morris divests Suzy of her coat and tells her to go play. He finds Jones and hands him a foil-wrapped banana loaf. Jones leads him into the kitchen, where a woman is talking on the phone.

'String him along,' the woman says to the phone. To Morris she says, 'Where's Suzy?'

'Hello, Lorelei,' Morris says.

'Fuck that,' Lorelei says. 'Where is my child?'

Morris goes to find Suzy. She's in the den, playing with a beagle. 'Time to go, Suzy,' he says.

Back in the kitchen, the only person he sees is Jones, spiking ice cubes from a tray.

'Where did Lorelei go?' Morris asks. He looks around the room again in case she is hiding, but there is only Jones. Morris feels the phone staring at him suspiciously, as though it still holds her breath.

'She left,' Jones says. 'She had to go shopping.' Jones and Lorelei are brother and sister.

Suzy got her blond from Lorelei, but Morris hopes that is the extent of it. Suzy blinks at Morris, waiting. She got her blue eyes from her real father, who is dead in Michigan. She got her vocabulary from Morris.

'Is everything okay out there?' Jones asks. 'I don't know a lot about parties. Are we doing all right?'

'Smashing, Jones,' Morris says. 'Smashing.'

Suzy soars back to the den, where the puppy is waiting for her. She pets the puppy. The puppy blinks. She scratches the puppy under the collar. The puppy likes that, too. She touches the puppy's ear with a fingertip. The ear flicks quick as a bug's wing, quicker than seeing. The puppy sneezes and Suzy is in love.

Outside, as the drinks go down, the guests start to slump a little less and throng a little more. A man standing near Morris points at the ceiling. 'Have I got this right?' he asks Morris. 'Is she actually dead up there?'

'I'm unclear on that point myself,' Morris says. 'You could ask Jones.'

'The guy in the kitchen?'

Morris nods.

'That man.'

Morris mingles. He meets the housekeeper, an Iranian girl with a long pour of hair on her like black honey. In the course of their conversation he learns she has no complete language. She was born in Tehran, but her family moved to Hamburg when she was two. At seven she was taken to Montreal, at twelve to Vancouver. Each language – Persian, German, French, English – was a box she tried to break out of, boxes nested each inside the next, like a Chinese puzzle. She is a delicious horror. Morris longs to lie beside her, to cage her in his arms like ivory and to whisper in her ear, beautiful things she will not understand.

Jones tugs on Morris's sleeve.

'Yes, Jones,' Morris says.

'She's dead.'

'What. You mean, now?'

Jones nods. 'What do I do?'

'What do you mean, what do you do?'

'With – it.'

They look at each other.

'That's a damn good question,' Morris says. 'Did you make plans?'

'Rio,' Jones says.

Morris stares.

'The other part, it kind of slipped my mind,' Jones says. 'Maybe if I get some more ice.'

'Suzy?' Morris calls. 'Honey? Start saying goodbye.'

He goes to find Shiraz – he has an idea that is her name – and asks her to come home with him and Suzy, but she says no.

Morris goes to find Suzy. When he picks her up, her breath in his ear is a thick whisper about chocolate. 'You and me both,' he says.

He is turning her into her blue raincoat when she stops, fists still poking the fabric for daylight. 'I want to see grandma,' Suzy says.

There is an interesting silence.

'Grandma's sleeping, pretty,' Jones says.

Morris can't believe it. Jones has a brain.

But Suzy is adamant, she is iron. She makes a break for the stairs and is snatched back by strangers.

'I know,' Morris says. 'Let's go for Chinese.'

'Hurray!' Suzy roars.

'Sssh,' Jones says, pointing upstairs and looking annoyed.

* * *

The first time Morris went for Chinese, he was six days old. His mother wore him on her chest in a tomato-coloured canvas sling. His parents were pathologically gentle people, walkers, sippers, smilers, tree-loving rainy-day pacifists, born fading. By the time he arrived, their lives were peanut-coloured, almost nude. In a baptismal moment his mother dripped sweet-and-sour sauce on his head, but she and his father were too engrossed in their respective fortune cookies to suspect meaning.

* * *.

His most vivid childhood memory was of sickness, which he loved. He loved staying in bed all day, reading books, eating Jell-O, flesh broth, globs of honey and aspirin crushed between two spoons. He loved the natural disorders of his body – vomiting, diarrhoea, infections, swellings, fevers, pale sleeps and altered appetites. Because his parents did not believe in TV and because he had a window, Morris watched weather. He saw blushing sunrises, curtains of rain holding in the night, snow in the blue afternoons. He missed prodigious amounts of school, was top of his class, and never wore a hat, in the hopes of catching something special.

* * *

In his bachelorhood, Morris would watch sports on TV. He watched blunt-headed events, car rallies and football. He watched women's triathlons from Hawaii, sun-slick virgins with space goggles and citrus neoprene and the strength of men. He watched figure skating. He listened to the hiss of skates, the music that didn't seem to fit with anything anyone was doing, the monsoons of applause. One afternoon he approached the TV and crouched before it, poked the skater gently with his finger and felt the prickling bite of static. She swooped and slithered. He studied her pixels. He imagined her laid out in his palm, a handful of dust. He imagined blowing her away. He backed away until she was a woman again, coronet and plumage. She glittered like sugar, like glass, spinning first one way, then the other. He couldn't turn her off. He let the afternoon go.

* * *

Morris once attended seminar in drag to see if anyone would notice. After graduation he got a job as a legal secretary. Eighteen years later he got stuck in an elevator with a crazy woman and her two-year-old daughter. He told them his joke about the zebra. It was the beginning of the end.

* * *

Lorelei the beauty queen had butterfly brains and the prettiest damn fingernails Morris had ever seen. She also had a baby girl who looked like she'd stepped off the top of a Christmas tree and was still floating down. They were like something from a magazine, and Morris wanted to cut and paste himself right into their lives. He braided himself then and there into their histories, so that a year later, when Lorelei, who was mad as a star, took off, Morris and Suzy were left in a twist.

* * *

Sometimes Suzy is pie-happy. Other times she is the pale queen on the dark shore, watching for stone ships that never return. At four she ties her shoes, recites the alphabet and dreams of winged men with glass hands that shatter and bleed. Ice is her favourite food. Morris puts food colouring in the ice cubes they eat together for a bedtime snack. He watches Suzy suck, then bite down. Her pyjamas still have feet. She is the black queen, pale and dolorous in her steel crown, mouth running with colours.

* * *

When Suzy is five, she and Morris attend a party given in honour of, or in spite of, the death or dying of Suzy's maternal grand-mother, Lenore. Death happens; trauma is narrowly avoided; bruised souls are slicked over with the balm of a good Chinese takeout and the inimitable joy of chopsticks in the hands of the uninitiated. Puppies are discussed.

* * *

When Suzy is thirteen, she and Morris will go to Jones's funeral. The service will be short and mercifully lacking in foolery – no poetry readings, mucus-riddled reminiscences or favourite pieces of cello music. Jones will lie quietly in his casket at the front of the church. On top of the casket will be propped a large black-and-white glossy, taken about fifteen years earlier, of Jones with a movie-star grin, syrupy eyes and feathered frosted hair. Morris will spend most of the service pondering this photograph. He will con-clude that Jones, being Jones, had it taken all those years ago with just this occasion in mind. Morris will surprise himself, at this point, by weeping.

Suzy will not cry. 'I don't get this,' she will say.

Jones will leave Suzy fifty thousand dollars, to be given over to her in a lump at the age of forty-four years. Jones will leave Morris wondering what space, if any, Jones's passing has left in the world.

* * *

When Suzy is sixteen and into black, Morris will overhear her talk-ing on the phone. 'This guy I live with,' she will say, meaning him-self, Morris. This will startle him, unduly, since it is only true.

Suzy will spend months of daytime in her room, door closed, blinds drawn. She never goes out; she never plays music. She has no boyfriends, girlfriends, clubs, interests or hobbies.

Morris asks her what she does in there.

'Think,' Suzy says.

'I'm trying,' Morris says. 'Yoga? Taxes?'

'No, that's what I do. I think.'

* * *

In university, Suzy will have a room-mate who dyes her hair black every two weeks to hide her red roots. The room-mate will have had an old Irish granny who told her she was damned to hell because she hadn't been christened. She said her hair was stained all the colours of sin because devils had crept into her mother's womb through the umbilical cord and kissed her scalp with mouths bloody from eating the flesh of the newly dead. The room-mate's parents used to go away for the weekend, leaving granny to babysit.

Suzy will tell Morris about her frantic spice-haired room-mate. He will tell her how he had always wanted a band called Dropdead Redhead.

'Was I christened?' she will ask.

'Absolutely,' he will say, wondering.

Suzy will write away for a copy of the parish records. One day a letter will come and she will burst upon Morris like a star, hurling a ball of crumpled paper in his face. 'They called me Candace,' she will spit.

'Well, look at it this way,' Morris will say. 'You're still a Pisces.'

'I am a fucking fish named Candace,' Suzy will say, her voice warped to a queerness, the closest she ever comes to tears.

Morris will wonder if he has ever loved her more than at this moment, his beautiful misnamed undaughter.

* * *

In graduate school Suzy will thrive, in a sick way, in her philosophy of science seminar. She will tell Morris how every scientific phenomenon has an infinite number of logically possible explanations. She will liken facts about the world to dots on a graph, which can be joined by any number of different lines, representing theories. She will tell Morris how human relationships are like scientific theories, where every fact one person has about another is a dot, but the connecting lines exist only in one's head. No two lines

17

are identical: love; a theorem; lines connecting lives; invisible threads looping through the universe, weaving a fabric of uncertainty and certain ignorance.

Morris will watch Suzy talk, Suzy of the black tunic and black leggings and the fine baby's hair. He will remember Suzy going into black, but he won't ever remember her coming out.

* * *

It is a fact about Suzy that she will never fall in love. People will come to her in fragments – a pleasing glance, the width of a hand, a tone of voice, a cast of thought – from which she cannot seem to cobble a passion. Or maybe it is that Suzy herself is fragmented, all shards and splinters, shivered by a world of farce and darkness. Or just that she is flawed: hair thinning like a banker's, and a coldness of bearing she cannot sense and cannot lose.

* * *

During a bout of food poisoning, Morris will come over to make Suzy ruby Jell-O and hold her hand. While she is in the bathroom throwing up he will look at her chick's hair on the pillow. Her hair is falling out.

When Suzy comes back she will look at the pillow. 'Oh, that Candace,' she will say.

* * *

When Suzy is thirty-six she will go to Morris's funeral. She will wear a baseball cap because her hair is many different lengths, and in some places absent. She will not change her clothes for the occasion. She will smell strongly of herself. She will not cry.

* * *

Fifty years later Suzy will be in her garden, weeding her borders. She will be remembering a time when she couldn't breathe if she saw a flower, when they were evil mouths that talked to her when she was alone, laughing and hissing, coloured cups brimming venom. How they waved their petals, furling and unfurling, blind twisting mouths, thrusting petulant lips. Now they will fill her head with a rush like rain, a song of threading voices. She will feel the grass about her, the looming blades, for she will have fallen – a stroke, they will say, sudden, they will say – and she will realize there was a time when she could look at a person's eyes and it was like looking into a house through an open window, and then when it was like looking through glass.

Days will pass before they find her. It will have been a slow death. Eighty-six years is a slow death.

* * *

Suzy and Morris in the Chinese restaurant, blue and gold. Through the window, the oriental filigree of traffic on a late afternoon downtown, after rain.

'This is how you eat an egg roll,' Suzy says. 'This is how you eat chow mein.'

Suzy is discovering chopsticks. She chews with her mouth open, concentrating. 'Oh, peas!' she says.

Morris looks at the goop in Suzy's open mouth. 'Here,' he says, passing her a plate. 'Some more of the green stuff.'

'Why?'

'It's good for you.'

'Why?'

'Eat.'

Suzy giggles and throws a pea at his head.

Morris giggles. Truly, he thinks, I am a terrible parent.

She throws all her peas at him, then pokes at her plate with the chopsticks for something golden and crunchy. 'Can I have a puppy?' she asks.

'Sure,' Morris says.

Always here, always now, he thinks, watching her eyes pool to glory. Always remember me this way. Because the day I am dust this is all you will have, and it will not be enough.

'Doggy bag?' the waiter says.

Suzy, alarmed, looks at Morris.

'Yes,' he says. 'Yes, please.'

STARS

'Is this looking like a panther to you?'

Elijah, Meredith's husband, was painting the archway over the new Adults Only section of his video store. Lily, Meredith's sister, looked on.

'It's a little humpy,' Lily said. 'More like a buffalo.'

Past the archway, in the old storage room, stood empty video shelves. Stacked against one wall were a dozen cardboard boxes, waiting to be unpacked. Lily had volunteered for this, since the boxes made Meredith furious.

Elijah stood on a three-step ladder. He had a gauze pad taped over one eye. He held a pot of silky pink paint. Pink like dawn over elephants, Lily thought. She liked Elijah very much.

'Meredith is so angry with me,' he said, studying the animal-shaped space he had left on the wet pink wall. Later he would fill in, black.

'May I browse?' said a man in a shirt and pants, peering past Elijah on the ladder, into the little room.

'This is my point,' Elijah said. 'This money, we need. Will we get types? I'm not saying we won't get types. Take this person here, for instance.'

'Excuse me,' the man said, affronted, walking off.

Elijah sighed and lifted the paintbrush up and down like a soup ladle, trailing pink threads. 'Please picture us as children,' he said. 'Your sister and I, just graduated from university, freshly wed, going into business. Beautiful movies, Fellini, Kieślowski, Kurosawa. This was two years ago. Do you know, for breakfast this morning, she called me a pimp?'

'She has a point,' Lily said.

The browsing man came back. 'Okay,' he said, holding his hands up like they were threatening him with a gun. 'Just, when does it open?'

Lily ate a wide, pale tortilla chip. Paper bags of these chips stood on shelves by the till, along with big jars of almond caraway biscotti and little jars of angry hot salsa, all home-made by Meredith. They had been her idea for stimulating business.

'Faith, hope, love. Never,' Elijah said. 'Tomorrow.'

Later they drained the neon, turned off the overhead set, and locked the till in the safe. They had to check the titles against the packing slip, make sure the movies were in the correct cases, and arrange the cases alphabetically on the shelves. They worked fast, smiling crookedly, like union elves.

'It's a whole culture,' Elijah said. 'Stars, suicides. I've been reading the literature.'

'Goodness,' Lily said, thinking of Meredith. 'What literature is that?'

He pressed three fingers against the bandage over his eye, as though to sop loose blood. 'Breasts can be arty,' he said.

She showed him one of the cases. 'Is that even legal?'

He blinked, inky-eyed, and took it from her. 'I told them not to send me this shit. I'm phoning Ray.' He held it up to the light.

'Ray'll take care of it,' Lily said, nodding. Elijah jumped up and bounded into the main room. She watched him lean over the cash desk and root for the speaker phone. Dialling out. 'Who is he, exactly?' Lily called.

'Ray!' Elijah shouted at the phone. Lily heard him laugh. 'No, I promise!' he said. 'She went home.' He returned to the little room, smiling. 'Well, Ray,' he said. 'You know.'

* * *

Ray was a tired man with a dirty look around his eyes. He had a leather jacket and the ghost of a handsome smile. He shook hands with Elijah but stood off from Lily, warily. 'How many of these you got?' he asked.

'I'm her sister,' Lily said, and then he shook hands with her too.

'Sweetheart,' he said, picking up a case and stowing it in a nylon sports bag, 'these slip in.'

Elijah went back to the cash desk. This time he closed his eyes and dialled by feel. He squeezed his eyes harder closed and mumbled. Lily couldn't hear. She turned back and saw Ray had been watching her watch Elijah. 'How'd you get into your line of work, exactly?' she asked.

He went on popping videos into his bag, nodding. 'Your sister asked the same thing, more or less. How did I end up as me? Women always ask, men never do. What do you make of that?'

'Men can imagine it?' Lily said.

'I used to deal, at university,' Ray said. 'I hate movies. I like cars. It's a cartoon life, what can I say?'

Lily waited. He had a tan, she noticed. Not so frail.

'You seem like a nice girl yourself,' he said.

* * *

Out of the store, into the dust and dead grass and gelled yellow sunlight of late afternoon, Lily walked where bees bigger than thumbs purred by her ankles, along the long highway, between the ditch grasses and the shoulder, until she got to Meredith's house.

'Have a good time?' Meredith asked, looking past her for Elijah's car.

Lily closed the door.

'I see,' Meredith said. 'He stayed behind to watch a few.'

'Oh, Merry. He did not.'

'He is most certainly watching some movies.'

Meredith had a floor-length robe and delicate hair. She collected books of photographs. They littered the coffee table like big silver pizza boxes.

'You're all dusty,' Meredith said.

Lily followed Meredith into the kitchen and watched her spoon sugar into a glass. She added a tea bag and a slop of milk while she waited for the kettle to boil.

'No more teapot?' Lily asked.

'You saw the bandage.'

'Can I have a bath?'

'You can have a bath.'

'Can I have an egg?'

Meredith eyed her reproachfully.

Lily got an egg from the fridge and separated it neatly into two wineglasses from the drying rack. 'You want the white?'

'Stop bothering me,' Meredith said, settling on the sofa with a vase of gin and a *Cinémonde*.

In the bathroom, Lily smeared the yolk onto her face with two fingers, glossing her eyebrows and the fine hair at her temples, avoiding her lips. She ran a bath.

'The boundaries of art are not at issue here!' Meredith called from the living room. 'Did he give you that line?'

Lily shifted in the tub.

'Alternative erotica my ass!'

'He didn't give me a line,' Lily called.

'I don't want to know!'

Lily got out, rinsed the egg smear from her face and danced with a towel.

'On the counter, in the blue jar?' Meredith called. 'I have some nice talc. Please don't use it.'

Lily went into the living room.

'Your face is all pink,' Meredith said. 'You smell like me.'

'Gimme clothes.'

In the bedroom, Meredith went into the closet and stayed there for a while. Lily tried on a pair of big silver mules. They stuck out from her heels like planks. 'Nice,' she said, clogging a little on the hardwood. She snapped her fingers, wound her wrists over her head, nose to bicep, eyes closed, and shuffled a spin. The dress hit her in the face – a sleeveless, backless bind of pale green silk with the finest zipper she had ever seen. It was cold to touch. She put it on.

'Don't sweat,' Meredith said.

Back in the kitchen, Lily tried to sit down in the dress while Meredith unplugged the frantic kettle and shoved her tea gear behind the toaster. She opened a tin, inverted a hockey puck of cat food onto a saucer, and collapsed it with a fork. 'You always liked Ely.'

'Yup,' Lily said.

'Dissuade him from those movies.'

Lily said nothing. She shimmered just breathing.

'Lucas!' Meredith hollered. Lucas was the cat, a patchy tabby with ripped ears and a pretty smile. He drifted in, star of his own silent film, and nuzzled the saucer. He took some meat into his cheeks and chewed. Lily wished she had a tail so she too could turn her bum to Meredith and trace such indolent arabesques of contempt.

In the living room, Lily and Lucas shared a chair. She wound a piece of her long hair around his paw. He kicked, yanking. He tried to jump to the floor and tripped, jerking Lily's head down. Her dress went crazy with lights.

Meredith shook her head as they untangled themselves. 'Only you could sprawl a cat,' she said.

They heard Elijah's Bug come chewing up the gravel driveway. A door slammed. 'You don't say,' Meredith said. They arranged themselves. 'Do you wax?' Lily asked.

Elijah stood radiant in the doorway, scratching his eyebrow with one finger. 'Women are bread and coriander,' he said.

'He watched the movies,' Meredith said.

He frowned accusingly at Lily, then brightened. 'Hey, you like my shoes?' She was still wearing the enormous mules.

'Ritzy,' Lily said, swinging her legs so they flapped and flashed against her heels. 'They're you.'

'Judas,' Meredith said to Lily. 'You just encourage him.' And to Elijah: 'Did we get any good ones?'

He went and knelt before her. He lifted her feet in his cupped palms, one at a time, and kissed them. He rubbed her arches with his thumbs.

'If I did one of those, would you take me out? Me and some popcorn?'

He decked her a look.

'Isn't he full of shit?' Meredith said.

'I like him,' Lily said.

'Oh, you,' Meredith said, vicious. 'I know all about you. When are you going to get a job?'

'Here we go,' Lily said.

Lucas spilled to the floor and ran. 'That's a smart cat there,' Elijah said.

The doorbell rang. 'There's Ray,' Lily said quickly.

'Oh, Lily,' Elijah said, and Meredith said, 'Oh, Lily, no.'

It was Ray. He had changed into chinos and a heathery grey polo shirt under his leather jacket. 'I found you,' he said.

Meredith put her fingertips to her hair, then let her arms drop to her sides. 'You've never even had a boyfriend,' she said, frowning.

Lily smiled at Elijah.

'She's trying to hurt me,' Meredith said.

'You're killing me,' Elijah said. His hand drifted up to his eye.

Ray leaned on the doorjamb, smiling at his feet. He seemed to be trembling slightly. 'Am I going?' he asked, looking at Lily.

'Lilian Gish, don't you dare,' Elijah said. He was pale around the mouth. 'Do you know what he is, really?'

* * *

Ray was a good dancer. He could anticipate. Lily danced like someone tossing hair from her eyes. Close up, she could smell the leather of his jacket. Later they walked down main street, into a crowd of movie-goers leaving a cinema. Lily still wore her sister's pale cool dress. People watched her pass.

'I'm going to call you Slim,' Ray said. He took off his jacket and gave it to her. 'For me, okay?'

She had been thinking of the time she kicked in the face of Meredith's TV, when she was first dating Elijah and bringing home all those foreign films. And now, as if an hourglass had been turned – the first skirl of interest, whisper of grit – a new suggestion of collapse, and the inevitable sly mounding beneath.

They walked for a while amongst the movie-goers, paired quiet as animals in the bright night.

HOUNDS

We live in a Moorish villa next to a cemetery. We are often informed that our villa, in architectural terms, is a folly. We know this. We live here anyway. We like it.

* * *

The Boy Scouts came to the door this morning. They were collecting for a bottle drive. This took us aback momentarily as we did not have a plan in case of bottle drives. The others had seen to all that, before they left. We told them we didn't think we had any bottles. They said the previous owners always had bottles. We said we could imagine that.

* * *

The previous owners were not the builders. The previous owners were a young couple in bad trouble with each other. The third time we came with the realtor, the last time we saw them, the woman took us around the side to show us her garden and how to tend it. Here are peas and here is basil and here are red currants and here is lemon grass. The words came through her mouth like they were of her body, not some public thing anyone could take onto his tongue, anytime he wanted. We liked this about her. We squatted beside her, conscious of the tender weight of the sky.

The man came out while the realtor went over the papers. She prickled in her skin when he looked at her. She raked the earth with her clean fingers, dragging up some weedy green with ripping lace roots, setting it on the grass.

The man says, Our suitcases are packed. Our house is in boxes in trucks. You don't have to do that any more. That's their job now.

Who am I hurting? she says.

Who are you hurting? the man says. You hate this house. Excuse me, she hates this house. Are we moving because you hate this house? Are we? So will you leave it alone?

Everyone hates this house, she says. Not just I.

Go wash your hands, he says.

* * *

We keep hounds. They are lean and smooth as water, always vanishing. We whip them the Frisbee out over the graveyard. They give pursuit. We are careful to play this game when there is no one around, usually early in the morning. We don't want to give offence. Once the groundskeeper was startled by the slipstream of a hound slipping by in the steaming dew. He looked straight at us. Since then we run the hounds at dawn only. After five a.m. we call them in and water them and talk to them about rabbits. We put the Frisbee away and they hang their wise slender heads. How do you explain a graveyard to a hound?

* * *

The Boy Scouts are back, out of uniform. So now they are just boys. They want to know if they can play with our dog. We say, Absolutely not.

* * *

Shortly after we moved in we were told, over a pile of pumpkin in the cold farmers' market, that our house was built at the turn of the century as a mausoleum for a rich man who had made his fortune importing blue cloth, but we knew this was not true. The builder had been an artist named, at first, Bob Johns. He had wanted to be an architect, excelled in Arches and Acoustics, but dropped out when he failed Stress. At that time he became Truck Stop, mixed-media artist and street performer – noodle juggler, cooked or frozen, depending on the time of year – and he commenced designing our villa. One of his pieces sold to the Metropolitan Museum of Art for a million dollars (or whatever it took to sustain the story) and he built it. Two years later he sold it to the couple and disappeared, spooked, the realtor claims, by the peace.

The dead don't bother us.

* * *

We wanted to decorate with silk and brasses, smoking lamps, scimitar palms and still pools. But you need women for such rooms, does with brown thighs and silver faces. Where do you get such women?

We settled for stars on the ceiling. We considered many different kinds of stars: Turkish, Phoenician, Lebanese. We endeavoured to work within the existing structural context – we gazed around. We chose ancient Egyptian. These are five-pronged or five-spoked stars, stick figures said to represent the souls of the lesser dead. They are simple and pretty and easy to stencil without too much dripping.

People used to like our villa.

Coming in, they'd say, Nice stars.

We would explain about the dead Egyptian stick men. They'd say, nice dogs.

We'd say, not dogs. Hounds, every one. Braces and braces of them.

They'd say, nice green grass. Peel-turf?

Nope, we'd say. Kentucky blue. This is one fast grass. Keeper mows it every morning and still it gets five o'clock shadow. Must be the soil.

People don't visit like they used to.

* * *

We watch the Scouts from the third-floor veranda. Scouting must drain them, for they spend much of their spare time, their boy time, lying in the cemetery grasses, smoking and resting. When the keeper comes out to chase them off, we know why. Sometimes in summer, at dusk, we sit out on the stoop and watch the services at the far end of the lawn. We watch golden motes, green grass blued by the turning light. We wish the boys could see this too. We drink a drink and watch the grief and colours down at the other end. We aren't morbid. We aren't cold. We know about redemption. We have a slice of faith.

* * *

Different visitors come now. Sometimes a sister, red-gold, bringing peaches. Sometimes a mother, dark and frowning.

What is in this room? the mother says. Why are all these doors locked? What happened to that wall? Why do you need a court-yard? What is this bell doing here? When do you plan to sweep?

★ ★ ★

Lately we have noticed the groundskeeper active with a shovel. He scoops and walks over and upends in our yard. We are fairly certain this shit is not the shit of our hounds, for we are ever vigilant with the baggies, but we don't care to press the issue. We also see him smoothing the earth over the new graves, earth strangely dis-rupted, night after night after night.

★ ★ ★

The Scouts come to the door again, as Scouts, for another bottle drive. We say, So soon?

They laugh, the Scouts. No bottles, mister? Got no bottles?

We say, We got cans. Want some cans?

Sure, they say, cans for a bottle drive. Ugly house, too.

Hey, we say. This is our house. We live here.

They say, You a meat-eater?

We've stopped answering the door.

★ ★ ★

A few days later the groundskeeper comes booming and pum-melling. Young man! he cries in the voice of his graveyard's God, I have called the Pound! This shall not continue! He declaims in tones so righteous even the hounds thump their tails in agreement. We sit in the innermost, windowless room, surrounded by our cans, listening from afar. We think of the boys, taking their ease in the long grasses. Oh, we can deduce. And this is not about hounds, although the boys and the keeper would have it so.

★ ★ ★

Reading the dictionary the other night, we discovered the meaning of the word 'houri': a young and beautiful woman of the Muslim paradise. We want houris.

30

Once we did have women here. They all looked the same, but, my God, there were hundreds of them. Plucked lips, pinked hair. In the bathroom they were slobs but some were handy, they fixed the truck, organized a recycling room. Others of them shouted. I'm not taking the dog out! they used to shout, and, What's so wrong with the radio? Still others were quieter – they brought us coffee and spent hours carving faces into pumpkins, out of season. We made pie of the innards and roasted the large seeds with salt in the oven. Pumpkin days, pumpkin nights. But then she'd be on about the radio again, why can't we have some music and what's so wrong with dancing now and just whom do you think will hear us, if you need it so quiet why don't you move next door? We were sad when she left but the realtor was right: some people can't abide peace.

But, houris. They could all look the same and we would still want a hundred of them. We would still want every one.

* * *

We'll admit, these days, to spending a lot of time in the recycling room, with its bins and shelves and orderly can piles. We sweep it out slowly and then we sweep it out again. We pretend we are caretakers wormed into the core of some vast factory, the only slow job for miles. We are an old man, we pretend, and the cans are a food source everyone has forgotten but us. When they are cold and queueing, we will eat black beans and apple sauce from the flat of a knife and drink bottled water. We will sit on a stool and smoke tinned cigarettes, rubbing the ridges of our hound's brow and pondering lapsed time, while outside they dash and shout and overlook this secret cache of plenty, and the old bugger nursing within.

* * *

Here is a conflict. We are running out of food. We used to have a lot of pork chops in the freezer, a whole pig's worth of pork chops, and cans of mushroom soup and some luxurious brown rice. That was a meal we were good at, but lately these things run low. We also like to mess around with canned tomatoes and tuna, garlic paste and dried macaroni. This is another of our meals, this noodle meal. We abhor – I say, we *abhor* – boxes. Now, even the hounds' food is canned. Three nights ago we fed them the last of the kibble. We folded the many bags and bound them with twine, like newspapers, and stacked them by the back door. The hounds come sniffing, rustling the empty kibble bags with their long soft noses. Watching us with their eyes.

* * *

The city slipped a paper under the door today. The city wants the hounds. The hounds want the paper. They lick, greedy hounds, they pant and sway. Last night we saw the boys making our problems, squatting and straining, pants around their ankles, shitting on their dead. Whose children are these? we ask the hounds. What race of men produced these? They lean on their picks, long moonlit metal. They look toward us and we believe they see. Scouts, we remind the hounds. Scouts, every one.

* * *

The hounds are getting hungry. We don't know what kind of dog they are, really. We know they're awake at night, they've been at the trash, they've been licking at the cans and some of them have cut their tongues. We see the blood on us when they come lapping kisses, snapping muzzles. They will blame the hounds for everything. They will blame the house. They could equally blame the Metropolitan Museum of Art or the gravity of the dead. I suppose each of us must start somewhere. But the next one who knocks, we will open. God help him we will open the door, for whatever comes next they will have asked for; and they will receive, bottles included, everything empty we own.

WATCH ME

Marie's brother called to tell her the junkies were gone.

'Since when?' she asked.

'Two days,' Steven said. 'But mum has their babies.'

'Oh, surprise.'

'I know, Marie, but two days. She says she's running out of activities.'

'Someone should report those people.'

'Someone did. Mum reported them to me and now I'm reporting them to you.'

'You know what I mean.'

'I know I'm going this afternoon and you're coming. Pick you up in an hour.'

'Oh, Steven.' She cut him off with the tip of her finger and poked her mother's number.

'Beth?' Laura, her mother, answered. Beth was the woman junkie.

'No.'

'Oh, Marie,' said her mother. 'Now, I wish you had been here for lunch. I made this pesto salad such that the curtains smell of garlic.'

'How are things?'

'Well,' Laura said. 'I'm surprised you can't smell it down the phone, it's that strong.'

'I can't smell it,' Marie said.

* * *

Steven stood in the doorway of Marie's apartment, wiping his glasses on his sweater. He held them up to the light and squinted and wiped them some more. 'Well, that's it,' he said. He put his glasses back on and looked at her intently for a moment, like he was testing them.

'No.' Marie sat in a wicker armchair, hugging a red cushion.

'Where's your pretty coat?' He meant her new anorak of vanilla corduroy.

33

'Mum dislikes that coat. Just go on your own.'

'Stop sulking,' he said, getting it from the closet and throwing it on her lap. 'She phones me because you act like such a goddamn groupie. You know I can't do this without you.'

Marie pushed her arms through the sleeves and reached into the pockets. 'I don't see what you're so afraid of,' she said, pulling on black leather gloves and making slow fists to work her fingers in.

* * *

Laura lived out in Langley, farm country a good two hours' drive from Vancouver. As they left the city behind the land opened up and flattened out. Marie sensed large animals, furtive cows and horses, fading in and out of the waning day.

'She just wants to talk,' she said.

'I know what she wants,' Steven said.

Laura was in her front yard, playing with the twins from next door. They had jagged translucent teeth and hot sweet eyes, like fudge oozing. They wore plastic boots, quilted space-suit overalls and miniature turtlenecks. Laura wore jeans, black rubber boots and their dead father's shirt. Her grey hair was stuffed up attractively under a baseball cap.

'You're just in time,' she said. 'We're going to shellac some gourds.'

The twins belonged to a couple of gentle junkies, Beth and Morty, for whom basic excursions – to the gas station or the supermarket – were perplexing epics. Often Laura found herself putting Natalie and Dylan to bed and getting them up again in the morning because their parents had run out of postage stamps.

'They're taking advantage of you,' Marie said.

'They're nice kids,' Laura said.

Steven had a soft spot for little Dylan. He taught him dog tricks. 'Come on, Dylan! Come here, boy!' he called from the end of the yard. Dylan loved Steven with the stupid love of small children. He romped over, grinning. Steven slapped his thighs, corralled Dylan with his forearms, then held a fist high in the air. 'Up, boy!' Dylan jumped, trying to reach the fist. 'Higher!' Steven ordered. 'Atta boy.'

34

Natalie studied Marie blankly before turning to cuddle with Laura. Apparently Marie lacked every appealing quality she knew to look for in her own species.

'Did you phone hospitals?' Marie asked, hugging her coat.

Inside, Laura laid some newspaper on the kitchen table and used a teaspoon to prise the lid from a tin of clear varnish. 'Here we go,' she said. Natalie and Dylan sat on the big kitchen chairs, smiling and breathing and kicking their legs. Laura dipped a pastry brush into the shellac and started to gloss a fat yellow gourd. She wore her wedding ring on her thumb.

'Beth and Morty went picking at Singh's,' she said in the slow, balanced voice of someone working carefully with both hands. Singh's was a strawberry farm.

'In that truck?' Marie said. 'That's an old truck. Anyway, it's October.'

Laura looked up at her and back at the gourd. 'We're going to do this,' she said. 'Then we're going down for the night. Let's just hold our fire until then. Steven?'

'Mum?' Steven said.

'I need you to look at the washing machine. It's thumping again.'

'Somebody needs to,' he said.

'Your father used to grease it with a little Vaseline, if you wouldn't mind.'

Steven went downstairs and Marie sat next to Natalie.

'We have certain responsibilities here,' Marie said.

'Don't start me,' Laura said.

'You're taking the easy way out,' Marie continued. 'This babysitting, for instance.'

'These ones, easy? Ha!'

'Ha!' Dylan said.

'Make the call, mum. You'll feel better.'

'Ha,' Dylan said, studying her.

'Hi,' she said. Natalie giggled.

'All right, you two.' Laura seized a twin under each arm and swept them, kicking and howling, upstairs. Marie picked up a science magazine with her father's name on the mailing label and began to read an article on robotics.

'I should cancel that,' Laura said, coming back into the kitchen a few minutes later. She opened the fridge and started pulling foods out and setting them on the counter. 'I never bothered.'

'Don't you dare.' Marie didn't look up.

'Pumpkin,' Laura said.

'Remember when he gave me that microscope? Remember how he was the only one who ever called me Molly? Can I have his slide projector?'

'I gave it to charity.'

'Jesus,' Marie said. She started to cry.

'Stop that, chicken,' Laura said. 'You have his armchair, his cushions, his good gloves, his antique typewriter and his bifocals.'

'I told you always to check with me first.'

'I have every right to dispose of my husband's things. Now reach me the cilantro.'

Marie didn't move.

'What did I raise?' Laura asked the ceiling.

Marie got the little wad of green leaves from a drawer in the fridge and dangled it under the cold tap while Laura skinned chicken thighs. 'Daddy hated cilantro,' she said.

'This is Aztec soup. Daddy loved this.' Laura slammed a knife down on the counter. 'Please go watch TV,' she said.

* * *

After supper they sat at the kitchen table and spoke like family.

'Your father never liked those children.'

'Daddy died before they were born. What's the matter with you?'

'He disliked them in the womb. Beth was sticking out all over at the time of the accident.'

'He did not. He did no such thing.'

'This does not sound like him at all.'

'There are lots of things you children don't necessarily know,' Laura said. 'For instance, to conserve water he refused to flush more than once a day.'

'You're making this up,' Marie said.

'It was worst in the morning, the smell but also the colour. Toilets full of yellow. I scrubbed and scrubbed.'

Steven said, 'Did you try the hospitals?'

'Marie's going to do it,' Laura said. 'She wants to.'

They sat her down with a realtor's pad and a pencil. Laura got the black rotary phone from the kitchen counter and plopped it in her lap. She and Steven smiled expectantly.

'You're only doing this because I'm studying law,' Marie said.

'That's right,' Steven said. 'We believe you can cope.'

Marie phoned and asked if anyone like Beth or Morty had been admitted. She listened and nodded a lot. She drew an abrupt line on the pad, making them jump and crane forward. 'Thank you,' she said, hanging up.

Laura said, 'Would anybody like some tea?'

'Well,' Marie said.

'I would,' Steven said, getting up to help her.

'Well, they're not hospital gone. They're just gone.'

'Banana tea,' Steven said, taking a box from the cupboard and shaking it next to his ear. 'What is banana tea?'

'What it says. You see, Marie, we told you.'

'They also said we should phone the police and report them missing.'

'Now, that's thinking.' The kettle screamed and Laura wetted the pot.

'No, it's not,' Marie said. 'The police will want particulars. They'll send social workers for the babies. Bloodhounds and social workers and forensic pathologists wanting DNA samples.'

'What?' Steven said.

'Blood, wool, cuticles, hair –'

'I can look after them,' Laura said.

'Not indefinitely. And I'm not sure if failure to report missing persons doesn't make this kidnapping,' Marie said. 'I'm not one hundred percent on that. But I think it might be.'

They looked at her, Laura with the kettle, Steven with the tea. 'Marie,' Laura said, 'one day you will have a good job with a pension and dental, and for that I am glad. But in other ways, law school has not made you a better person.'

'I am trying to think ahead,' Marie said.

Laura looked at Steven.

'We'll stay tonight,' he said. 'Tomorrow we'll take a drive into town and check it out. We'll ask some questions.'

'I suppose you'll want to camp in your father's room.'

'Trying to plan,' Marie said.

'Come on, citizen,' Steven said. 'Let's scout some sleeping bags.'

'I'm going to lie down now,' Laura said. 'I'll leave the phone on the hook, but you people have tired me out.'

* * *

Their father's study felt like a sealed room in a shipwreck, fathoms below real air, with its low ceiling, its buttery yellow tone and its fireplace full of books. During the day, the only possible sunlight came from a single window near the ceiling, a rectangular frame stuffed full of colourful glass bricks the size of ice-cubes.

Marie got a heavy glass tumbler from a desk drawer and a bottle of Scotch from the mantel. Next to the bottle was an ornamental pepper plant, dripping waxy red peppers – inch-long, kinked like fingers – in a flare of matt gold foil. The plant was new and made her hungry. She poured a thick finger of Scotch and rinsed it around the glass, then set the glass down. She took the plant and placed it on the floor in the hall, just outside the door, peppers trembling. She took a shoebox down from the bookcase.

Steven came in with an armful of bedding. 'Help me with this?' he said. She set the shoebox next to the stereo. They laid out red sleeping bags and white blankets and pillows in two rough bed shapes, taking up most of the carpeted floor.

Marie got a deck of cards from another drawer.

'Steven,' Laura called.

'Coming,' he called back, looking at Marie.

'You're okay,' she said.

'I know.'

'She just wants to talk.'

'I know. I know she does.' He went upstairs.

Marie took a cassette from the shoebox and hinged it open. On it her father had printed 'Evangeline Ray, June 1967'. She tipped the tape into the stereo and clicked a finger panel. A woman began to sing jazz about her man. She sang deep and clear and behind her voice people were coughing and scraping chairs. When she finished there was a splash of applause.

Marie sat on one of the made-up beds. She tilted her drink back and forth, watching the play of glass-light in the loose white wool. She adopted a yoga position, pressing the glass between the palms of her feet, and leaned forward to deal a hand of solitaire. When the tape ended she put in another one. 'Hello,' her father said. 'We can't take your call right now, but please leave a message after the tone.' She was still listening to the tape unwind its silence when Steven came back.

'Feel like a hand?' Marie asked.

'I feel like taking a trip,' he said. 'Do you feel like that?'

He pulled down a magazine file stuffed with maps and BCAA guidebooks. He spilled the pile across the sleeping bag between them and took the glass from between her feet.

Marie picked up one of the books and flipped through it, half reading about campgrounds and restaurants and inns in southern Alberta, half watching as Steven unfolded a map. He looked surprised as it got bigger and bigger. He looked up at her as though she might be thinking the map was his fault.

'So?' he said.

'Head-Smashed-In-Buffalo-Jump,' she read. 'The Badlands. Hoodoos.'

'Hoodoo you think you are?'

'Sip,' she said. He gave her the glass. Upstairs the phone rang.

'She's thinking about planting runner beans next spring,' Steven said. 'She's going to give everybody earthquake survival packs this year for Christmas. She's worried the Civic won't make it through AirCare.'

'The Civic is okay,' Marie said. 'She barely drives it.'

'That's not the point.'

'Steven,' Laura called.

'That's the point.'

'Stay,' Marie said. 'I'll go.'

Laura was sitting up in bed, quilt pulled to her chin. 'Oh, Marie,' she said. 'Could you please get me a glass of water? It's just that my hip. I didn't want to get out of bed.'

Marie went into the bathroom and rinsed Laura's tooth mug. 'You did too much today,' she called over the water.

'Those children are little energy packets. Where's Steven?'

Marie came out and handed her mug of water. She squinted at Marie's chest. 'Bunny, I wish you wouldn't wear your father's clothes. Are you cold? I'll lend you a sweater.'

Marie didn't answer. Laura turned her head to the window. Her lips tightened and her eyes changed. Marie peeled the sweater off and stuffed it under the covers. 'Here,' she said quickly.

'I have some nice clothes,' Laura said. 'Perhaps when I'm dead you'll want to wear them. That was Beth on the phone.'

'Where are they?'

Laura threw back the quilt. The chunky brown sweater lay against her knee. She shook it out and pulled it over her head, over top of her white nightgown. 'Home.'

Marie looked at the window and saw light in the house next door, sudden yellow rooms scooped from the darkness.

'You children get so angry,' Laura said. 'Steven won't let me touch him, and you act like your father's pencils are shards of the true cross.'

'We miss him.'

'I don't know what you miss. You don't act like children.'

'We aren't.'

Laura rose slowly and pulled her jeans on. 'I've made a decision,' she said, sitting back heavily on the bed.

Marie got Laura's runners from the closet and knelt before her, loosening them. She fitted them onto her feet.

'One more night. Just until morning. They're asleep now, anyway.'

Marie didn't answer.

* * *

'Do you think she's shooting up over there?'

An hour had passed. Steven and Marie sat on the sleeping bags playing war, a card game that involved throwing the deck at one's opponent at strategic moments. Steven had the jack of clubs propped in the bridge of his glasses, while Marie rose periodically to refill their drink. Lena Horne was torching on the stereo, loud.

'She's arguing with them,' Marie said. 'She wants to keep Natalie and Dylan.'

'She needs a pet.'

'She needs two.'

Steven threw a handful of cards at Marie. They fluttered down around her head. 'I see your two pets and I raise you a husband.'

Marie picked the queen of hearts out of the Scotch and licked it off. She held it up to show Steven. 'Ha,' he said.

'Where do we get one?'

Steven cleared his throat and tucked his chin into his chest. 'Examine this rationally,' he said in a deep, bored, familiar voice.

Marie giggled. 'Method, children,' she drawled.

'Remember that Scotch is the drink of the educated man.'

'And, due to the shape of his thorax, Zoot Sims was the greatest saxophone player of all time. This is scientifically provable. The zenith of Western music was Billie Holiday's mouth.'

Steven laughed, then brushed the jack of clubs from his forehead. Laura stood in the doorway, holding the pepper plant.

'It wasn't so much he didn't like them,' she said. 'But he was so afraid they'd be born addicted.'

'Everything OK over there?' Marie asked.

Laura held up the pepper plant and twisted it side to side. 'It's like a little Christmas tree, isn't it? What are you playing?'

'Cards,' Steven said.

'I offered to keep them for another night, but they said I'd done enough.'

Marie turned off the stereo. She made a show of standing up – pulling her jeans straight, brushing off imaginary sleeping-bag lint. She was drunk. 'Excuse me, I have to make a call,' she said.

The kitchen phone was whacked black plastic, cracked and venerable. She knew that phone. Its receiver offered tiny tunnels to hospitals and light.

'Who are you calling?' Steven had followed her upstairs.

She stared at the back of her hand, the one that wasn't gripping the receiver where it lay in its cradle. 'Police,' she said, frowning.

Steven sat down opposite her. He reached over, pinched the jack out of the back of the phone, and held it up like an explanation. Marie relaxed but said, 'Gimme.'

'They came back, Molly. They're right next door.'

'Don't call me that.'

'Molly, Molly, Molly.' He squinted at the plastic jack, then waved it in front of her face like a tiny cobra head. 'You are feeling very, very sleepy.'

'No, I'm not.'

Steven let his hand fall to the table. 'Me either.'

'Where's mum?'

'Down there, fixing our beds.'

'What's wrong with our beds?'

'They're *fine*,' Steven said. 'She's just making them even *better*. Are you sure this is a 911 thing?'

'No.'

'We should call somebody, though.'

'Definitely.'

'Even though they came back.'

'It doesn't matter that they came back,' Marie said. 'What matters is they went away.'

Steven took his glasses off.

'Drugs are bad,' Marie said. 'This is how bad drugs are.' She looked up at the kitchen clock, at its five-minute slices of pie. 'You'll still love me, right?'

The fridge fan rattled off, leaving a ticking quiet. Steven reached over to plug the jack back into the phone. 'We all love each other,' he said. 'That's how these things start.'

THINGS

The hall outside her room smells of piss and cigarettes. I ask her if she's ever tried to quit. She looks amazed.

She says her name, Calla, is short for something. I ask: Calla lily? Calypso? Calliope? Calpurnia?

She says, None of that.

She wears pink tights with a bloodstain down the inside of one thigh and a white sweatshirt that says Moon Society in black block letters.

Calla lives in 2C. The other tenants want her to leave.

2B is an old German named Axel Kempf. He was a tennis instructor. He made training films. One year he made it to Vimbledon. He wears sleeveless white v-neck sweaters and white open-necked shirts with the sleeves curled up to show his tan, his sucked-out muscles.

I live in 3A, a studio, my first room away from home. It's white and small and I keep it clean.

* * *

In the grocery store I buy tortillas, juice, milk, condoms, soap. I worry the cashier will write to my mother and tell her I buy tortillas, juice, milk, condoms, soap.

* * *

Axel in his doorway says, Hallo Fräulein. Look, this is me.

Photograph of a soldier with a tennis racket, smiling forever.

He looks at my limp T-shirt, frayed shorts, stubbled legs. He says, I like to see a slim girl in a sundress, so you can see her back. Why have you all stopped wearing dresses?

* * *

Inside my fridge: milk, yoghurt, kiwi fruit; Parmesan shaker, unopened; grapefruit, whole.

My mother phones to give me the recipe for That Lemony Chicken I always wanted on my birthday, and to remind me not to trust men. She asks, have I written this down?

I'm on the floor. I lean my head against the wall, close my eyes and say, Garlic, rosemary. I close my eyes and look out the window.

My friend is an archaeologist. He likes bones. Dinosaur bones, Neanderthal bones, ribs from the Chinese takeaway. When I am Egyptian he brushes me with his brushes, my flesh his dust. When I am Siberian he ladles warm water over me, thawing me slowly. I open my eyes. My mother says, Just remember: if it's pink inside, it isn't done.

* * *

I meet Calla on the stairs, trying to eat a hamburger and drink a shake and carry two takeout bags and walk upstairs and breathe, all at the same time. She says, What's inside there?

Violin, I say. Oh, you mean – yoghurt.

I like yoghurt, Calla says.

I practise in the basement, where the laundry machines thump and tick. I draw lines in time. Afterwards I lie back on a pile of warm towels and work on my breathing. I watch tufts of insulation between the rafters.

Axel says Calla makes sounds at night: wall-slams, monkey laughter, moans.

* * *

I meet Calla in the grocery store. She says, I can't find the hair jelly. I need some.

I take her to the right aisle and help her find the shelf. She takes a tube, unscrews the cap and squeezes some green into her palm. She smells it and smiles. Oho, she says. This is it!

Now we are friends.

* * *

Axel in his doorway says, Hallo Fräulein!

Photograph of his dead wife. She wears a hat. He keeps her in a pretty silver frame, delicately traced with swastikas.

Americans make it rhyme with 'gnat'. The English make it rhyme with 'snot'. Germans rhyme it with 'nut': Nazi, like a kind of Christmas cookie.

Axel says Calla keeps him awake.

* * *

Calla has a social worker named Pippa. Pippa has a braid. She gives Calla sample budgets and meal plans, and encourages her to go on outings with the Group.

Calla brings her sample sheets to my door. She says, Macaroni and carrot sticks? Whole-grain banana loaf?

Also, Calla dislikes the people of the Group. She says they make too much noise at bus stops.

* * *

My friend tells me he is going to Turkey for a year. I dream I'm flying a toy plane. Turkey is a sandbox with cocktail palm trees and lemon-coloured hills, studded with tinfoil minarets. I reach down and touch the hills. They warm my palm.

* * *

My mother phones. She says, Your life is green. It's a young green life. But you sound thin. Should I check on you?

* * *

I find Calla sitting on the front steps, eating doughnuts from a paper bag and crying. There is white powder around her mouth and her tears are making tracks through the powder.

Calla, I say.

Now she's wiped her hand across her mouth and got snot halfway to her ear and powder in her hair and her mouth open crying, dripping food.

Calla, I say. Come inside.

I walk her inside and up, her eating all the while and howling, face leaking. Axel opens his door and says, Unglaublich. This is not human.

Calla's room smells of toast and monthly blood. I look at the garbage pail and look away. I open a window.

He shouts at me, Calla says. He talks backwards.

She lies down on the bed and curls up, pulls herself to sleep.

Back in the hallway, Axel says: I know you are a musician, but you must have less feelings. Look at this skinny girl with her violin. Are you Mother Teresa? What can you do for such a one?

* * *

I decide to buy Calla a present. I buy lemon soap and lemon tea and thick wool socks the colour of slate. Walking home, I realize I want these things for myself.

Under my door, a petition for her eviction. I read *decency, odour, unreasonable.* I fold the paper neatly and place it in a rustling white plastic grocery bag containing furry stripes of kiwi peel, six useless condoms, a bag of mouldy tortilla.

* * *

Axel in his doorway says Komm, komm, Fräulein. You must come in. See, I have made cookies.

The light is yellow. The wall behind the TV is postered with the big blue Alps. Shades are drawn. Candles, pine.

He holds out a star-shaped foil tray. Jam, chocolate, ginger, almonds, spice. A fire in the hearth. On the table under the window, four lit advent candles. Their smoke sends four brass angels with trumpets swirling under a five-pointed star. Outside, it's the month of July.

If an archaeologist opened the top of Axel's head, like an ancient tomb, and spooned out the contents, here is what he would find: a doll's tennis racket, a two-inch Christmas tree, tinfoil bells, insects playing Bach. Each fragrant with the zephyr of second childhood, gingerbread and urine. Warming it all, a tiny golden hearth of hatred for Calla.

I say: I have to go. I have practise.

His mouth inverts, clown-like, a circus wound.

* * *

Inside my violin case: violin, bow, resin, cloth, Band-Aids, moisturizer, spoon, postcard of a camel.

Flip the postcard: he digs in a residential area for the skeletons of ancient children. He says the Turkish housewives throw kitchen refuse into the pits for a joke. As if he would take a chicken carcass for a bone-baby. A fish for a child.

Axel leaves a gift in a brown paper bag outside my door.

★ ★ ★

Fight evil. Ask Calla to come to the park.

Calla says, Can we stop at the grocery store?

Swallow. Say: That's a good idea.

In the store, say, Those nectarines look good. I'm going to get some of those nectarines. Would you like some too?

Calla says, I want chips.

Look at Calla and think of my flesh grown lush, bones sunk back down inside.

Sit on a bench in the sun. After her chips Calla has three nectarines and a cigarette. I watch the sky.

We leave the tongued stones, sucked to tidiness.

★ ★ ★

A few nights later I wake to a slow throb of lights, colours lapping my wall.

In the morning comes the landlady smelling of coffee, broth. We had a little incident in the night, she says. Old Mr Kempf got into that Calla's room, ranting about melons. Police took him off in a cruiser.

I imagine Calla sitting up in bed, long hair loose, sweatshirt streaked with toothpaste dry and white as bird shit, clutching her bedtime snack of cookies with icing, medications, and a can of cola to wash it down.

Maybe he told her she was fat as melons.

In my fridge the milk has turned. I swirl it down the drain and rinse off the smell. The kiwis have bruised to a poisonous sweetness and colours crawl across the yoghurt. I tip it all away. I am afraid to take a knife to the grapefruit, of the rot unfurling inside.

Maybe he told her guts were wet and red like the inside of a melon.

I scribble out music, looking for sweet tones, feeling like an insect: the thrust and whine of my bow, my proboscis.

Get out. Pass a woman with a cat on a leash. Danzig was a bad cat, the woman says. He peeped on the lino. Is that a violin?

I imagine her wound up in soiled sheets, shocked as Mary by this vision of a man who sees through to her bones and still will not let her be.

Maybe he told her about the killing of some prisoners, how their heads came open like melons. Maybe he looked at her and said, Forgive me. There was nothing I could do. Am I still your child?

* * *

Calla is gone. I ask, Did they take her away?

No, says the landlady. She left. She paid the rent and she left, and she took her unchristly smells and behaviour with her. Do you know someone who wants a room?

* * *

He phones. I say, where are you?

49

He says he can see a pizza parlour, a mosque, and a block of flats. He says he can see a boy with a basketball, a woman in a chador, gum in the gutter, power lines, a crescent moon. He is at a pay-phone on a street in Ankara, at dusk. The sky is waiting to pounce.

In the background I hear a seagull. I say, Was that a seagull?

He says, I need something from you.

Inside my garbage: tortilla, yoghurt cup, condoms, soap, kiwi peel, chicken recipe, petition, socks, tea, brown paper bag of sand-butter stars and gingerbread bells.

I imagine sending it all to him with a note saying: What do you make of this? Now, now do you see what absence means?

SEXY REX

Our most unusual wedding present – a golden retriever – comes from my mother. On the first night of our honeymoon, spent in the new old apartment Monica has painted five shades of blue, we can hear him rattling outside the bedroom door. Distracting – did she intend this? And all this first summer, as the sky snaps and spits electrical storms, we get in from work, drink wine in the dark, kiss on the fire escape, and wait for the dog to come home. He pulls these all-nighters now. We've started calling him Sexy Rex.

We're both twenty-four, both going to be engineers. Monica shops and I cook. I phone my mother. 'Okay, baby calf liver,' I say, reading the tub.

'Very, very foolish,' my mother says.

'At forty-nine cents!'

'And he wonders why? Fry it to leather and feed it to Sexy Rex.'

Monica works at the airport, for Canada Customs. She spots heroin, guns. I drive a florist's van. Summer jobs, but we've got our eyes on the future.

I phone my mother again, later that evening. 'We've just made wills,' I say. 'We've both decided, no heroic measures.'

'Very wise,' my mother says.

'We're leaving everything to each other. After that, over to you.'

'I don't want your junk,' she says. 'Do you even have one Stones album? You have nothing I want.'

'We have RRSPS now,' I say. We do. 'You can have all Monica's clothes.' She's sitting here now, in her flowered T-shirt and a slip-silk sarong. She smiles at that. 'Any time.' She smiles more.

'How was the meat?' my mother asks.

'I sautéd it in a little olive oil, with onion and rosemary.'

'Did Sexy Rex like it?'

'Dog *loved* it,' I say.

* * *

One night last Christmas my room-mates and I gave a party. I knew Monica vaguely from Fluid Mechanics. I invited her; terrifyingly, she showed up, so I ignored her.

'She's going to sit over there all night kissing that beer unless you go talk to her,' my room-mates said.

She had her hair fisted up into a tortoiseshell claw. There she was, with her sweaty beer and her plain girl's pretty smile. Here I am, reminiscing at twenty-four. Meanwhile Sexy Rex is out there somewhere, taking his time in the eager republic of dogs.

* * *

'Lentils,' I say.

'A six point five degree of difficulty,' my mother says.

* * *

Working at a florist's, I steal flowers, of course. One day from the cooler I snag three witchy black roses.

She buzzes me up to her condo and answers the door in a belted black suit, wide white shirt collar overflapping the lapels. She's so seventies, she's nineties. Monica and I, we decided last night, are *nouveau* eighties – Greek food and mutual funds, Venice.

'Frank Sinatra is dead,' my mother says.

'Long live Frank Sinatra,' I say, but my mother shakes her head impatiently. '*It only just sank in.*'

In the kitchen, here and there, she has pasted neatly laminated CD covers to the tile: *Miles Smiles, Mingus Antibes* '60. 'Cool,' I say, and it is.

'Yeah, what the hell,' she says. She's in the mirror posing with the roses, a grim corsage against her heart.

My bride puts the marigolds in jam jars, in the sunshine, in the morning. Life is *long*, I think suddenly. Where is the dog?

* * *

Wife in the kitchen sunlight, burdened with groceries. Motes of dust and anger and sun. 'You were supposed to walk him,' she says.

'He walks himself, these days.'

'If you lost my dog,' she says, voice trembling now. This is the last thing she says for quite a while.

I phone my mother. She says brightly, 'What's for supper?'

'Oh, I've got *steak*, over here,' I say. 'I've got lemons and crusty French bread and little Moroccan olives and *cocktails*.' I tell her about the vanishing of Sexy Rex, and my newly Carthusian wife. 'Three days!' I wail.

Silence, dark and deep.

* * *

'You are such a dog.'

Flat on my back on the sofa, my mother in the kitchen, my bride pouring gin, I should disagree? We found Sexy Rex after two hours, two blocks away, dirty, happy, trying to play hoops with some kids with a pretty collie. Now he is clean and fluffed from much brusque brushing by Monica, on the floor, tasting my out-flung fingertips.

'You're lazy, you can't cook, you steal, you lose my dog,' she goes on to say.

'But you've got your voice back.' She swats me with a dish-towel. Oh, beautiful doghouse.

'Supper is almost ready,' my mother says, appearing in the kitchen doorway. 'I'm doing this for the first and last time, please note. This is a one-off.' The apartment smells of wine, beeswax candles, delicious char and juices. Plus mom's perfume, wife's baby powder. 'I thought my useless son was joking about the steak and the drinks.'

'In the store, I don't know what came over me,' Monica says. 'It was a moment of weakness.'

'I love moments of weakness,' I say. Sexy Rex whumps his tail, *yes!*

They shoot me looks. I love their looks. They put their heads together, conspiring to feed me, train me, love me, punish me. *OK, I'm a dog*, I think, closing my eyes, scenting my women and the food-fragrant air.

TEA DRINKS

Finally she takes me aside to tell me you just can't treat people that way. This is in the garage, behind the house. I try to look preoccupied. I finger the blade of my jigsaw, frowning.

'These are our friends' children,' she says.

'OK. Fine.'

'At their age, they're emotional. I'm not saying *you* have to be emotional.'

'Fine.'

'It's nice back here, isn't it?' She looks around, bats some dust hanging in the window-light, making it swirl. 'Smelling like sawdust. All your tools around you.'

'Cold,' I offer, as a reason for her to go back inside.

'Coming?' I ignore. Her eyes narrow, her face sharpens up with the memory of why she followed me out here. 'Knock first, is all I'm saying.' But she softens again, watching me rub the blade with a rag.

'Goodbye, Ellen,' I say.

And she's this dumb, her eyes are this blue: she says, 'Where are you going?'

Where I go, I go to Roy Campbell's, two doors down. 'Oh, man,' he says, shaking his head when he sees it's me on the doorstep. We grin. I glance over my shoulder like there's someone waiting for me back in the street. He ducks at the knee to get a view of the sky. The day is cold and echoing like iron.

In the kitchen Jolie is sitting at the table looking at the table. I lean down to kiss her cheek and she says, 'Get away from me. You're cold.'

'What are you doing?' I say.

'We're trying to think of baby names, still,' Jolie says. 'We're trapped in this downward spiral. What's a good girl name?'

'How long have you got?' I ask Roy.

'Two weeks?' Roy says. When he hands me my coffee I can smell he hasn't showered yet.

'Twelve days,' Jolie says.

'You know it's a girl?'

'We don't know that,' Roy says.

'Well, we do, honey,' Jolie says. 'The ultrasound technician let slip.'

They look at each other, a stand-off.

'What have you got so far?'

'Nothing,' Jolie says. 'I'm serious. Give me one girl's name.'

I look at Roy, who shrugs. 'Michelle.'

'Oh my God,' Jolie says, burying her face in her hands. 'See what I *mean*?'

Next I go to the store. There's a wind now, a genuine winter wind sending last night's scurf of snow whispering along the pavement with me. I wish I had my jacket and gloves. When I get inside I stand for a few moments rubbing my hands, hoping one of the sons will shoot a friendly comment my way. After all, I am a regular and they are Italian.

After a minute I take a basket.

'Tomatoes,' Ellen says when I get home. She's unsacking my purchases, cans, on the counter. 'And – tomatoes.'

I tell her about the father, with the plum-like bruise under each eye, who does the reckoning in his head and takes your change from a tin box under the counter.

'Well, I mean, I know,' Ellen says.

Our house guests are in the dining room in matching terry robes, crowding each other over the newspaper. 'You can't help!' Delia says when she sees me, covering the crossword with her hands.

In the den their son Stephen is playing advanced Minesweeper on my very big new computer. He's playing slowly – calculating, tiptoeing, playing to win. I can respect that.

'Sorry about that bathroom thing,' I say.

He ignores.

Ellen tells me he is going through a break-up and he is suffering and I should try not to make things worse.

Ellen has joined the guests back in the dining room. Tom is still with the crossword; the two women have their legs under them, chatting. Ellen is telling Delia about the father with the plum-like bruise under each eye, who does the reckoning in his head and takes your change from a tin box under the counter. 'GST and everything,' Ellen says, tapping her temple.

'Well, as you know, we have a new house in the suburbs,' Delia says, gripping her robe together at the throat when she sees me. 'It's not, like, an ethnic neighbourhood. But we like it.'

'Delia, you idiot,' Tom mumbles, erasing something off the crossword. '*Sekhmet*'. The phone rings. When it rings a second time he looks up, annoyed, and says to Delia, 'Phone.'

'Phone,' Delia says to Ellen.

I take it in the hall. 'Is Stephen there?' a girl says.

I tell her she has the wrong number.

In the kitchen Stephen's little brother Max is finger-filching brown sugar from the canister. Max is a prize. For twelve he is, how can I say this nicely, fat. When he sees me he says, 'Fuck.'

Tom and Delia have assured us Max does not have Tourette's.

'Want a cookie?' I ask.

Max breathes through his mouth. Max says, 'Fuck, yes.'

How can I put this? I like this kid.

'Want to play Minesweeper on my new computer?' I ask him.

'Stephen is.'

'Yes, he is,' I say. 'He's taking your turn.'

Max blinks, then he gets me. He grins. In addition to the fat there is the crew cut, the pig nose, the button-down shirt. The kid reeks of 1957. How does he do it?

'Bring the box,' I suggest.

In the den Stephen has his elbows on the desk, chin on his fists, considering the screen. He makes Minesweeper look like philosophy. When we come in he sighs.

Max slaps the cookie box down on the mouse pad, jiggling the game. 'My turn,' he says.

'You could have asked me first,' Stephen tells Max. 'You didn't have to get him.'

The phone rings again.

'Stephen *Morrison*?' the girl says. 'I think he's staying with you?'

'Is this the famous Karen?' I say. Stephen turns to look at me.

'Oh, my God,' the girl says contritely. 'I'm totally bugging you, aren't I? Only he said it would be OK to call. Is this a really bad time?'

Stephen is on his feet.

'Give him a minute,' I tell Karen. 'He's going to take the extension upstairs.'

Max has already installed himself in my desk chair, killed his brother's game, and started his own. His game is more like mine: fast, random clicking, playing the odds. He kills three starts this way while I wait for his brother to pick up the phone in Ellen's room.

'Karen?' he says finally, his voice loud and intimate in my ear.

'Oh, my God,' the girl says. 'Is this terrible? Should I not call?'

'Wait. Has he hung up yet?' Stephen says.

I hang up.

'That Karen?' Max says. 'I saw them fucking one time.'

'No kidding,' I say.

He turns around to look at me. 'It was ugly,' he says, and I realize the child is telling the truth.

'Your brother is a pretty morose guy,' I say.

'She's got him by the dick,' Max tells the computer.

In the living room, Ellen says, 'We waited and waited.'

'Where are they?'

'Getting dressed.'

I sit beside her on the sofa and take her hand. 'I don't want to do this any more,' I tell her.

'Well, no,' Ellen says. 'Me either.'

'All of it, I mean.'

She drops my hand.

'Sorry,' I say.

'Was that the phone just now?'

'Guess who.'

'They're so mature, talking about it. Delia says she's never seen him like this.'

I wander over to the newspaper, dispensed all over Ellen's grandmother's table. 'Matriculate,' I say. 'Six letters.'

'Delia says she hears him crying in his room at night.'

'I invited Roy and Jolie over for drinks later,' I say.

'What drinks?' Ellen says.

I look for the pencil. 'Tea drinks.'

Delia knocks on the doorframe, announcing herself, like she doesn't want to sneak up on us. She's wearing, that I can see, socks and jeans and a green Roots sweatshirt, my guess a men's size large, which she doesn't need.

'Delia wears such big clothes,' I say, smiling.

'Talk to you?' she says to me.

I put the pencil down.

'Stephen says would you please not eavesdrop on his phone calls.'

I look at her.

'OK,' she says, patting the door frame where she knocked a second ago. She goes away.

'This is what I mean,' I tell Ellen. 'This is exactly what I'm talking about.'

'Really?' Ellen asks, frowning.

Tom sticks his head through the archway. 'Look,' he says to me. 'Don't give Max cookies.'

I pick up the pencil.

'I realize we're guests,' Tom says, staring at my pencil hand.

Stephen jogs down the stairs, looks in at Ellen and me like he's checking the contents of the fridge, then turns to Tom. 'Dad, is it OK if Karen comes over?'

I look at Ellen for confirmation.

'Of course,' Tom says. Stephen goes back upstairs. 'Can you get her off the phone, though, son?' Tom calls after him. 'I need to call Foy.'

Foy is the fumigator.

Delia rushes in, pointing at the window. 'Excuse me, I'm sorry, but is that snow?'

'Oh! Hot chocolate,' Ellen says, straightening her back.

The sky is white. Some flakes are drifting.

'Honey,' Delia says to Tom, business-like.

'Well, I'm calling Foy right now,' he says.

'They said seven the earliest,' Delia says. 'But if it's going to dump I'd rather set out immediately. We can sit in the driveway until it's safe to go in.'

'At least then you know you're home,' Ellen says sympathetically.

'You can loan us blankets, right? Hot drinks? For sitting in the car?'

'Damn that Max,' Tom says.

I'm indignant. 'What'd *Max* do?'

'We blame Max,' Tom says. 'From one day to the next, roaches. It's too coincidental. It would be like him. Hey, you know what? You guys could go check the weather channel for us.'

'We can do that,' Ellen says, grabbing my arm and pulling me away.

In the den the boys are playing the computer together. Max has the mouse but Stephen is directing operations. When Max clicks Stephen flinches.

'Boys,' Ellen says. I click the remote for the TV.

We find out we are expecting twelve centimetres by midnight.

'Well, I don't know what that means, exactly,' Tom says.

Delia holds her hands apart. 'Five inches,' she says. 'Like a candy bar.'

'Boys!' Tom calls.

'I'll get the thermos,' Ellen says.

I say, 'What about Karen?'

Everybody looks at me.

'He's right, hon,' Tom says to Delia, still looking at me. 'We'll have to wait and take her with us.'

'Yeah, but,' Delia says, looking out the window. 'Well. OK.'

It's snowing now. It's started.

An hour later the doorbell rings and Stephen jumps for it. But he comes back, not with some snow-dusted cold-fragrant fairy waif, but with Roy and Jolie. Roy's hair is damp.

'What's your name?' Jolie asks Delia.

Delia looks startled. 'We're not actually staying,' she says, automatically reaching for Jolie's coat, and for a moment I wonder if she's going to put it on and leave.

I find Max still at the computer.

'They think you smuggled the roaches into the house,' I tell him.

Max looks impressed. 'How'd I do that?'

I'm studying what he has on the screen, a game I've never seen before: little balls you fire at a wall from a mortar, pinging out bricks. Each colour gets you different points. 'I have this?' I ask him.

He's staring at me, waiting for an answer.

'Little jars?' I say.

He looks awed.

'So, out there, we have these guests now,' I warn him.

In the kitchen I arrange everything for tea. When I take the tray into the living room Ellen gets up to help me. 'Stop disappearing,' she whispers, frowning.

Stephen is standing beside Jolie's chair. When Ellen approaches with a mug he takes it from her and turns it around so Jolie can take it by the handle.

'So, *Ellen*,' Jolie says. I can see her tasting the name.

'Jolie,' Ellen says.

'Surviving?' Jolie says.

Ellen smiles at me. I say, 'Hi, Jolie.'

'Get away from me,' she says. She looks around for somewhere to put her mug without getting up or leaning forward. When Stephen reaches to help she cocks a thumb at him and says, 'Can I have one of these?'

'He's my Stephen,' Delia says.

Stephen does bashful. Then he does troubled. He says, 'Karen should be here. I mean, it's taking too long. I'm getting worried.'

The women sigh.

'*Karen*,' Jolie says pensively.

Roy shakes his head.

'Karen, my girlfriend,' Stephen says.

Everyone looks at me.

'Nothing,' I say.

Outside a snowplough goes too fast down the street, orange lights flashing on the snow, blades up. Everyone turns to watch it recede.

'Why?' Delia says, anguished.

'That right there I would call the point of no return,' Tom says.

As an afterthought he looks at his watch. The snow is wafting now thick as cotton flock. 'That's it, folks. Ellen, looks like we're staying another night.'

'That's why it's called a recliner,' I say.

Everyone looks at me.

'Everyone know how old Stephen is?' I say. 'Folks? Stephen is fifteen.'

'How come you're always coming over to our house?' Jolie says. 'Ever since Ellen moved in. You know you can't do that after the baby's born. You're going to be stuck here.'

Ellen straightens her back and smiles.

'You two are going to have to work it out,' Jolie says.

I look at Roy, but he's staring at the front window. Outside, a light-haired girl in a puffy ski jacket is standing in the yard, shading her eyes, looking in at us.

Stephen sees her and slowly touches his hair.

'Don't let her in,' Ellen says.

Nobody moves.

'The air's no good in here,' Ellen says.

Jolie puts a hand on her belly.

We watch Karen bite off a glove and tick on the window pane with her fingernails. She's saying something. *Stephen*, she's saying, you can see from her lips. She waves, smiles. Nobody moves. Her pretty brow creases. *What!* she says, just below the threshold of audible. Behind her, a tree branch tips off a snow clod, leaving a trail of powder in the air.

'Karen's here,' Max calls from the den.

When Roy moves his head his glasses catch the light, turning his eyes into white ovals.

Karen points inquiringly at the front door, then wades out of sight, arms up for balance. After a moment the doorbell rasps.

We wait.

Max thumps sockfoot into the living room. 'Karen's *here*,' he says. 'She's ringing the door.'

Nobody moves.

'Fucking rude,' Max mumbles, knuckling one fat fist in his eye, and gets the door himself, to everyone's amazement but mine.

SONG

Two boys went into a house. A girl waited in the car.

* * *

It happened like this. The boys went into the house while the girl waited in the car. When they came out the girl drove them away. For some time it wasn't clear to her what had happened.

Shit, whispered the one. Shit, shit. He was the younger one, with straw hair and an intemperate personality. He sat next to her in the front.

She herself was sweet on the older one, who sat on the back seat. He kept his hands in front of his face and appeared to be praying or thinking hard.

Did you get? she asked. But the boys wouldn't talk to her. They weren't talking at that point.

Names – Craig, Marco, and Sherry.

Sherry was sixteen then, Craig fifteen. Marco was eighteen. These were facts. At trial, no one disputed that Sherry stayed in the car.

I got some on my pants, Craig said as she drove. Hey, man. Will you look at this.

Marco leaned forward to look over the bench seat.

* * *

It happened like this. Sherry imagined an old woman who lived alone. She would be frightened and give them her money.

* * *

It happened like this. Marco knew of a widow, the mother of a man who had once ripped off his father. The man had shaken a fist in his father's face. He had ripped up an invoice and laughed. His father wouldn't care about this old woman or what his son might do to this old woman. She would be sleeping, and wake to find

63

vengeance had been and gone and robbed her blind while she had been sleeping.

* * *

Craig didn't give a fuck.

* * *

Two boys went into a house. The girl waited in the car. She felt sick. She tried to remember why money had seemed like such a good idea, what she wanted it for. CDs? Lipsticks? I don't want any more lipsticks, she thought. She sat in the car with the engine running, the exhaust going up like a white signal, thumbtacking them to the map of the cold curved street.

They walked out slowly. Marco closed the front door behind him and gave it a little tug to make sure it was locked. Neither of them was carrying anything.

* * *

It was Craig's idea, the electrician's tape.

* * *

It was Marco's idea, the electrician's tape. Sit still, he told the old woman. She was crying. He hated to touch her skin. He wound the tape around her wrists, behind her back, round and round, binding rather than taping, freeing the tape from the roll in snatches. Craig had gone down the hall to the left while Marco did this thing. This was fast. This was happening fast.

* * *

No hurry now, she remembered at trial. Craig or Marco had said it. One or the other.

No hurry now.

What happened? she asked. She was driving. They were a ways away and she wanted to know. How much did –?

Sherry, said Marco.

There was a smell. She caught it then.

Oh, she said. You.

64

She stopped the car. Craig fell out his door and threw up onto the ground.

It was him, Marco said. It wasn't me.

* * *

Craig went down the hall to the left while Marco tied her up in the kitchen.

The curtains were drawn in all the rooms. The beds were made. It was like underwater. He didn't want to go in the rooms, didn't want to take anything any more. He wanted to go through the motions so as not to anger the older boy, and then he wanted to leave. He felt nervous and guilty. He knew what he was doing was wrong. Yes, he was afraid of violence, he was afraid. Yes, he was afraid.

* * *

Marco went up the stairs to the right while Craig watched the old woman in the kitchen. He was looking white so Marco didn't try to get him to do anything. When Marco went upstairs Craig was just standing there looking white. Marco had given the old woman a cuff to keep her quiet and told Craig just to stand there and not do anything. The cuff was nothing, like you would deal a puppy.

Upstairs the carpet was thick and pale and took the imprint of his steps like stains. He had to drag his feet to smudge them out. There was a bedroom with a cheap computer and a small bathroom with a sloped ceiling. He wasn't taking much in. He heard a sound like a puppy and headed back down the stairs to get the younger boy out of there. It had been a lot for one day.

* * *

She waited in the car.

They had been to the beach at White Rock, the three of them. This was the day before. Sitting on a picnic table overlooking the wide sands they had teased her, calling her a Surrey girl, which meant slut. It had been nice sitting there in the open with the ocean and birds in the air and a boy she liked and the three of them laughing. They didn't know each other very well, except that none of them felt like going to school that day or the next.

* * *

It happened like this. The boys were shouting at each other while she drove. She couldn't understand it. Finally Marco said, Stop the car.

He got out and slammed the door hard. He started to walk, he started to run toward the intersection. He ran against the electric hand telling him not to cross and they saw him slam his palm down on the hood of a car which had had to brake hard for him, almost at his hip. He ran out of their sight.

He hit her hard, Craig said when Sherry looked at him.

When she looked back at the street she saw the vanilla man come on for the walkers as though to say, That's right.

It was him, Craig said. It wasn't me.

* * *

Before they went into the house they had each kissed her for luck. They must have talked about it beforehand because she was not expecting it and afterwards they were both smiling and would not look at her or each other. The blond boy had done it first, shyly on the cheek, and then the dark boy. He had leaned over the back seat and touched her ear and when she turned to him he smiled and touched her hair and kissed her mouth. Then they got out of the car and proceeded up the front path to the house, smiling at nothing at all.

* * *

Craig was abused.

* * *

Marco was abused.

* * *

Sherry was abused.

* * *

Two boys went into a house. There were knives in the sink, knives in a block, knives in drawers. The hands of the clock were a knife and fork. There were knives in the bathroom, knives in the bedroom, knives in the carpet and knives hanging from the ceiling.

Forensic reports revealed a single weak blow to the head and seventeen stab wounds to the back, neck, and head. The knife was a poor choice, blunt and serrated, probably a steak knife.

Marco tried to think what would anger him least. Good boy, he said. He was sure that was what he had said, watching the blade in the other boy's fist. You did what you had to do.

Craig tried to think what would anger him least. Shit, he said. But he couldn't speak after that. The older boy had put the knife down and grabbed him to stop him falling. That was how the blood came to be on his clothes.

They washed at the sink like brothers, or unlike brothers.

When Craig got his knees back under him they got out of that house. It had all been pretty quiet but Marco locked the door behind them anyway, just to slow whoever came next.

* * *

Before they went into the house they had each kissed her for luck. They must have talked about it beforehand because she was not expecting it and afterwards they were both smiling. The older boy put his face to her ear and bit her while the younger one leaned forward to kiss her on the mouth. She felt tongue, teeth. They were both at her at once and then they were gone, out of the car and proceeding up the front path to the house, walking straight and tall with their animal heads like something horrible out of Egypt.

* * *

The sun had slipped from its place in the sky. This was the day before. Sherry was getting cold. They sat on a picnic table at White Rock with their collars up against the cold, smoking and talking quietly as the last daylight pooled in the ocean. Her hands were white and cold. Christmas was coming.

The idea had been with them all that day and they had enjoyed talking about it, planning it and taking themselves seriously. They each wanted a little bit of money, that was all, for little things they each wanted.

* * *

It happened like this. As Marco came down the stairs he saw Craig standing behind the woman tied to the chair. Both had their backs to him. Craig was leaning forward and then Marco saw him unsheath the knife from her body. That would have been the last time, number seventeen. He had had to stab between the railings of the chair. Her clothes were black with it.

* * *

It happened like this. When Craig came back from the bedrooms to the kitchen he saw what at first seemed to be a badly applied coat of red lipstick on the woman's mouth. She was still tied to the chair. The older boy was behind her, leaning forward as though to whisper in her ear. Then she started to drool and it was red.

Later at the sink when he saw the older boy wash blood and particles from the knife he started to cry.

* * *

Two boys went into a house. At trial she would be asked whether one or both of them had acted strangely that day or before. Meaning: which one and why?

The younger boy had tender shadows under his eyes and a childish temper, subject to bizarre triggers – seagulls, hunger, kissing. He had flown into a rage when he caught Marco laughing with Sherry behind the White Rock 7-Eleven, his little face all twisted, almost crying. He had gone in to buy liquorice while they waited outside but when he came out he couldn't see them right away and thought they had taken off.

Marco had carved obscenities into the picnic table with a Scout knife while Craig and Sherry ate the liquorice. Then he tried to sink the knife to its hilt in the wood of the table. He and Craig took turns gripping and wiggling it, trying to work it in deeper while Sherry ate the liquorice. It was somewhat stupid behaviour, she thought, but it did not detract from the sweet thing she had for Marco or the general good feeling of the day.

* * *

Two boys went into a house. Marco knocked on the door while Craig looked over his shoulder.

Don't, Marco said.

The door opened. Yes, the woman said.

Marco leaned down and hugged her. He picked her up off the ground in a hug and carried her into the house. Craig followed, pulling the door closed behind him. Anyone watching would have seen a young man giving an old woman a nice big hug.

Don't you hurt me, she said. I've seen your faces.

* * *

Two boys went into a house.

Don't you hurt me, she said. I'm not afraid of you.

As he came towards her she cried out but he walked past, behind her back, like he was going upstairs.

* * *

It happened like this. Sherry was alone in the car.

She was driving down Hastings Street in the blue hour when tail-lights are rubies and people are feeling good. She had felt good herself yesterday at this time at White Rock when they saw the streetlights come on like someone switching on the night. That was a hundred years ago. Now this thing was in between. She realized her life would be divided now into before and after.

Two boys went into a house. What happened? She tried to imagine. It happened like this. Two boys went into a house. She looked down at the passenger seat of the stolen Jetta and saw long stains. Carefully she signalled and crossed into the slower lane. She signalled again and parallel parked and pushed the gearshift into Park and ratcheted up the handbrake. She turned around to look at the back seat and it was there too. It was then she saw the electrician's tape snatched from the roll, the aquarium light of the bedrooms, the footprints in the carpet, the hands of the cutlery clock, the black clothes and new lipstick, and the boys leaning down each in turn as though to kiss or whisper in her ear.

But I was in the car, she thought. I was in the car. I was in the car. I was in the car.

Across the street glowed a payphone with a white light both harsh and soft. She went to it. Soon she could hear the long rising praise of sirens. Much later, after the prescribed period of tales and contradictions, her companions were duly convicted, the younger one as a child, the elder as an adult, and they were sent to different places. Two boys went into a house – yes they did.

At trial, she wondered if he still liked her.

JOE IN THE AFTERLIFE

Joe has been kicking his daughter out of the house since she was three. He can't help it, she's annoying. He shouts, but she whips books and cups at his head. Now, twenty years on, she's retreated to the bathroom as usual – violent, shaking, trying to get back inside herself. He likes it when Gaby loses control of her body like this, when she's angry.

Ellie, Joe's wife, has asked him to stop evicting the child. 'I'm leaving anyway!' shouts the brat in the bathroom. This is not news. Gaby lives half packed, waiting for the planets to align and the bluebirds to sweep her to a bachelor with hardwood and cable for four-fifty a month, in a gingerbread house with a chocolate landlord, on a major bus route through the enchanted wood. 'I'm serious,' Joe tells Ellie.

Still, they have this fiction, or he does, that she is leaving tomorrow or the next day.

The days have been coming up hot. Six a.m. generally finds Joe in the back garden with tea and *New Yorkers*, in the tiny cooling slivered between night and day. He sleeps poorly, melancholic that he is, but enjoys the weightlessness of dawn. He floats up on it, and spends the rest of the day falling.

This morning Gaby appeared, eyes poached from sleep, airy-fairy in her little-girl nightie, with its ribbons and stitching. Had he woken her, nabbed her magazine, scored her mug?

'I dreamt a man was having his arms chainsawed off,' she said.

'Oh, please,' Joe said.

He knows what she needs. Her progress was arrested, he reckons, back in the creature stage, when she was supposed to learn to socialize with the other little crawlers at play school. But she got to books early and became a person while other people's offspring were still engaging little geckos. Now she won't leave the house. The stuff she collects for her apartment might as well furnish a tomb for the afterlife. Nothing gets used.

'You don't like anyone,' he said once.

'I like Sam Cooke and the Hollies,' she said. 'I like Gandhi.'
It's 1999. She needs a little push.

* * *

Later that morning, Joe steps out to taste the air. Gaby has her
futon frame on chairs in the garage. She's stirring a pot of urethane
with a foam brush. The milky liquid looks too thin to have a purpose. 'Don't come stand over me, Daddy,' she says.

'Mum thinks you might like our bread knife for the new place.
Is this true?'

Gaby wants to start painting, doesn't want to be looked at. Joe
knows. 'Oh, it's no secret I covet that knife,' she says.

'What is that stuff, milk?' Joe asks, turning back to the house.

'That's right,' she says.

Reaching for the doorknob, a pain in his arm stops him like a
question. Are you sure? it asks. He's on his knees before he knows
it, on his face. He or Gaby is laughing. Both, he thinks afterwards.
Both, please?

* * *

Live on television, tethered astronauts are aloft, soundlessly patch-
ing their craft. The film lurches – intimate, faintly obscene – like
film of insects.

Gaby sits beside him, absorbing images from the set. He's in her
room, in her bed. He never allowed her to move her bed from her
ground floor room to the attic loft and now he's in it, so.

An English nurse, bright and worthy as a new penny, comes and
goes like a toy. She reminds him of the ambulance. That was a
sunny day. A black flower had bloomed in his brain.

But will you look at this, Joe thinks, picking at an old, ongoing
argument in his head. His daughter is an ascetic and a cold, cool
woman. The walls and curtains are blue, the bookshelves are
another blue. The girl herself slumps in a wicker armchair, puffed
with cushions styled from a blue silk sari – *Ellie's* craft and thrift.
Blue shadows puddle the corners. Otherwise the room is picked
clean of personality, like a hotel room between guests.

And here sits Gaby, in her sandals and army surplus pants and the inevitable white T-shirt, no makeup, no jewellery, no graces at all, hugging her legs to her, mouth mashed to a knee, eyes on the set. He finds her easier to love in the summertime – small, impatient, muscled like a boy, strung up and down with blue veins. But she has an RRSP, which he finds ghoulish in a young girl with good skin.

He's so sick, he realizes.

The pennyworth nurse wears a cardigan, pink or green. After she leaves Gaby makes fun of her. She takes Joe's pulse. 'Bloody marvellous!' she says. 'Now touch your pain.' He can't much move, can't smile, although she's doing it for him. 'Brilliant!' she says.

Ellie brings food for each of them on a tray. She and Gaby eat spaghetti with chicken and olives. Joe sips the spoonfuls of gelatine she slips between his teeth. There is a machine in the corner between the bed and the wall, heavy and square, set down like a piece of luggage. No one pays it heed except Joe, who would like to know if he is attached to it.

Days have been flipping past, like cards; and their black backs.

The sickroom curtains are drawn; the TV is alive. His wife and daughter wear lovely flickering masks. He wonders where the astronauts are going. When he makes a sound to ask they slowly turn, they look at him in wonder.

* * *

The speech therapist wears a smart, creamy little summer suit with a daft sleeveless polka-dot blouse. When she removes her jacket he sees her arms are richly tanned, all the way up to the shoulders. He approves. She is after his heart with her careless skin – not like his own pair, with their fears of sun and estrogen and God knows. Although, to be fair, both he and his wife come from cancerous families. Barring the unforeseen, Gaby can expect to go that way, as Joe himself had expected, until now.

The speech therapist sits beside him on the bed and makes a business with flash cards and tape recorder, propping items on his leg. He feels placid and coddled, unfocused by her lovely skin. He senses her growing urgency – his hand squeezed, names repeated.

His eyes swim in the dots on her blouse. Her throat too is nutty, her jaw, ears. Silver knots peg the lobes. What a lovely, babbling brook of a stupid woman. All right, he thinks. Just a minute.

He watches her mouth form shapes and his tongue butts tooth, trying to wet his dry lips. She disappears behind his head. *It's too soon*, or *It's no use*. The astronauts, stiff as big gingerbread men, don't speak clearly either. Their efforts emerge as radio cracklings in Houston. 'Roger that,' says Houston.

Gaby never turns the set off. She seems to need CNN like morphine. Is this what she does, long hours alone of a Saturday night?

I don't care, I think she's a lesbian, Joe told Ellie last month. It's fine with me. Safer in every direction when you think about it. All I'm saying is, at her age, she should be getting *out*. The astronauts give way to the death of a rock star, shot once accurately by the husband of a deranged fan. The fan had abandoned her family to stalk the singer, although at one time the whole family had been fans.

His daughter seems to hunger for this stuff. It lights her up, makes her laugh. When they play the rock star's famous song she hums along, snapping her fingers to the beat. 'This is for my dad,' she says, and sings the chorus into the microphone of her thumb. When the shot cuts back to the astronauts, she pounces towards the set, pointing. 'The empyrean!' she cries.

Ellie looks in. 'Gaby,' she says.

At first, Ellie is there at night, eating raisins and reading *Anna Karenina* and books about paint. The phone rings, giving her a start. 'Curses,' she says, picking raisins off the carpet. The phone rings too many times – won't she answer? The TV stays off at night and he misses it – imagines the pulse behind its bland black eye. *Stay*, he thinks often, of no one particular. Shapes in his mouth, sweet and pepper – *stay*. Nights are as usual the worst, a despair of small sounds. It's summertime, again or still, the progress of summertime, and the insects – their fine Swiss mechanisms – bother his reason. Gaby emblazons them to the walls with a slipper, not often enough. Saltwater sleep – he tries to get back under. But a mosquito has found his name and is repeating it, in its tiny tight language, over and over.

* * *

Gaby has started a diet, a thing he has never permitted. His mind's eye follows her to the kitchen – ripping up lettuces, drinking water as an appetite suppressant. Thinner than *what?*, he thinks, fretting.

The astronauts are down. There have been brochures, lately. Lately she has been showing him pictures, too close to his nose. 'It's a dorm, Dad,' she says, shaking her head. 'There's gonna be ivy.'

Now she upends a sack from the drugstore onto his knees. Small, shaped items click against each other, coloured sticks and circles. She opens a compact and shows him a neat flat square of, apparently, hot chocolate mix. 'Eleven ninety-five for dust,' she says. She powders her nose, then his. She pops a lid and squirrels up a tube of lipstick. In a minute she looks like a small child who's been eating fruit. 'All right?' she says. She wipes it off and tries again.

And then it's liquor store boxes, boxes, boxes. She and Ellie have spent the day on the floor taking kettles in and out of paper, it seems like, telling each other to put the books in small boxes and where is the list and thank you, thank you, you're sure I can take it?

'No one drinks coffee here any more anyway,' Ellie says.

I can buy a better one, Joe tells himself. I'm sick and I'm rich. I can have anything I want.

* * *

Time flows and overflows. 'Goofs wear make-up,' says the brat at the mirror, expertly now at the mirror, pinking in her lips. He looks at the loot from her jeans pockets, the precious piles – pennies, nickels, starfish of keys. She puts it all on and takes it all off, with tissues and puffs and costly waters, until her face is pure again. She sorts her boxes. The TV is alive.

* * *

'What did the doctor say?'

He hates his own voice, such as it is now – the animal speaking-sound he makes, all sonorous wadded tongue.

75

'I'm anaemic, for one thing,' she says. 'He says it's like I gave blood, but every day. He says I have to take supplements and eat, basically, more.'

'*Uh*,' says Joe.

'There's nothing like a soiled urinal to get you thinking about the future,' Gaby says. 'Personal hygiene is a long and winding road.'

Ads. She rises to a protest of bones, body static, and lopes, stretching, to the bathroom.

On the television, beautiful women are selling creams with their beauty and naughtiness. They wink and lightly finger their faces. Their decadence is ancient and irresistible. Even Gaby is a sucker for their balms. He once hated her – *hated* her – for buying a little cake of complexion soap for thirty dollars when she was fifteen and her skin was poor. Imagining *what?* But he thinks now of the old woman's body she carries about within her gradually revealing itself. Take care of her! She's here now! Eyes, voice, baby pudge, eaten by aliens! Skin tortured, voice transposed down, hands buckled and sheathed with arthritis, sure as Christmas. He wants her to get out there, get married, now, soon. What's your problem? he thinks to his child. Marry a man, marry a woman, what are you waiting for?

He seems to recall his own wedding, but with a deluxe, five-star wealth of detail that falsifies the memory. Ellie in her wedding dress, spitting in the garden. Guests flinging palmfuls of pins. Ellie in her wedding dress, in the hotel room, talking on the phone, nibbling her bouquet. Gaby already known, there in her little spaceship, inside Ellie. A single black seed, like a kiwi seed, lodged in his brain, behind his left ear.

Either he's getting better or he's getting worse. That, he realizes, is the answer.

* * *

Kiss. Doors slam. Gaby leaves.

After she's gone, Ellie decides to stencil the walls around him, to keep him company. She has low-odour paint. On the second day she abandons the template and goes freehand. *She's drawing on the walls*, flowers and such, twining lines up near the ceiling. She stands on his bed to reach her pencil into the corner, tracking and trailing graphite down the blue walls, her foot nudging his hip. On day five, frowning like an artist, she abandons her paints for a single colour, gold.

* * *

A speech therapist comes to the house, a West Indian woman in a white suit with a giddy tropical blouse. They make sounds at each other, smiling, and she leaves him with exercises. She will come each week until he is better.

Ellie no longer sits with him at night. It's cool and dark and dry in this painted room, with the whirr of jewelled insects exploring his daughter's woks and socks. Tonight they watched a program about space exploration. The narrator was lucid and seemed to peel back the mysteries of distance and light; Joe hoped children everywhere were watching. When it was over he felt like a steady ship. But then he asked, 'How long have I been down?'

Ellie looked at him. 'Three weeks,' she said. 'Including today.' What was she waiting for?

A door opened in his mind. 'Where does Gaby sleep?'

'At the dorm.'

Now, alone in the dark, this answer he finds familiar, although he knows it to be false. She is in the next room, of course, or the next; he can hear her fidgeting at night, like the princess bedded down with her golden pea. Her tiny sounds, tiny rages and incoherencies. Presently she will come and watch TV with him, as she has always done, cool in her skin, his little alien. He has her now.

Comforted, he floats on down summer's river, royalty inspecting the desert.

LETTERS AND NUMBERS

It had been a fragile blue egg of an April Sunday, and I thought if I could get past it the summer might be all right. In the morning I washed the truck, and most of the rest of the day I spent on the sofa, or going to the window to check on my big vehicle gleaming on the sidewalk. The truck I had bought when I was working, with the trick money of earnings – money that replenished itself month after month, fooling me into a sense of my own worth. But lately I was living on real money, savings, and liking it. On savings you can see how many days you bought as a regular citizen, and how many days, as yourself, you may spend.

In the evening, my friend Sam and I went to a basketball game. He said he wanted to get me out of the house, but really he was after a cheerleader. The game was in the gym of the local Catholic high school. There were a lot of dating couples, a TV crew, families with squirts of kids, and young men in wheelchairs. The evening was laying down light like carpet.

'It's wheelchair basketball,' Sam said patiently, as though we'd been through all this before. 'Michele's boyfriend is captain of Saint Jude's.'

'You said basketball,' I said. 'You didn't say special basketball.' Some kids turned around to look at me. 'We came here to steal a cripple's girlfriend?' I asked.

We gave our red paper tickets to some kids at a table and took seats in the bleachers. A few were already rolling around down there, dribbling and shooting. A giant crucifix hung over the East hoop. The fans were happy and knowledgeable.

'This right here is both a genuine sport and a happening scene,' Sam said.

People were clapping and making whoo-whoo noises, so I leaned forward, elbows on knees, and did some clapping of my own. 'Hey hey hey!' I called. Before me, a girl with boy's hair and chunk earrings held her hand out to the court like a traffic mistress, explaining something to her friend. A snack boy clambered

79

over the bleachers with a laundry basket full of warm hot dogs wrapped in tender foil. I bought two dogs. A priest blessed us from centre court and the game began.

'There she is,' Sam said.

She was blond as a little girl. It was wrong, wrong, what he was there to do, and I decided to help him fight it.

'She shits out of that ass,' I said. 'Little poky hairs grow under that skin.'

'You anus,' said the man on my left.

'I have love,' said Sam on my right.

'You Catlick?' said the man on my left. 'I hate Catlicks.'

After the game we went with Michele and the boyfriend for burgers. The boyfriend's name was Rem. Although his team had won, he still looked intense. He had muscled brown arms, enviable arms. He pulled an olive sweatshirt over his white T-shirt and put on a navy watch cap. He was a strong, good-looking, unhappy man in a wheelchair. He and Michele drove in his car, a retrofitted charcoal-and-black Accord. Sam and I followed in my shiny truck.

'Rem is interested in the paranormal,' Michele said over beers.

'I have a master's in cognitive science and abnormal psychology,' he said.

'Rem, what kind of name is that, Rem?' I asked.

'Dutch,' Michele said. 'Tell them about Boston.'

'I've applied to do doctoral work in Boston.'

'The brain is some fancy meat,' Sam said. Michele looked up at him.

'In Boston,' Rem started.

The food came. We had all ordered burgers except Michele, who got a plateful of shells and surgical implements.

'Clam?' she said, pronging one and whiffling it under Rem's nose. He batted her hand away. The table came up to his chest. I could see he was used to this and it bothered him. I thought about what I had noticed on the way in, how one of his feet pointed at the other, and wondered what he could do and what they could do together. I bit my burger, thinking about his spine.

'Why, thanks,' Sam said. He took one of Michele's buttery mussels between his thumb and fingertip and hoovered it into his mouth. I started talking to Rem.

'What,' he said when I finished. He was watching Sam, who had a fry ringlet on each finger and was waggling them at Michele, who was laughing. She took a fry from his thumb and ate it. 'Athletics, what?' Rem said.

I excused myself to the john.

'Who brought the hermaphrodite?' I heard him say.

The men's had a concrete floor, five stalls and a single functioning, buzzing, seizure-inducing fluorescent over the furthest sink. I wetted my hands in some dubious gold water.

Sam came in and stood next to me, studying his charmed self in the mirror.

'Why am I here?' I asked.

'You're doing great,' he said. 'She likes you. You're clinching the deal.'

Sam's hair stood up in a crest and his eyes were bright. 'Sammy, Sammy, don't do this,' I said.

Back at the table, Rem and Michele were laughing. It died out of them. Sam and I sat down.

'I left something in the car,' Rem said abruptly, and spun himself off into the parking lot.

'He's got a present for me,' Michele said.

Sam swirled the truck keys on his finger. He had talked them out of me in the john. 'Yes?' he said.

I felt hatred for those two rising in me like a Venus from toxic waves, Venus with black breath and terrible posture. Through the plate glass window of the restaurant I saw Rem watching us. After a minute he jerked himself over to the door and back to our table. He was flushed.

'My car's gone,' he said. We looked at him. He smacked his palm down on our table and his voice got louder. 'My car's been stolen.'

'Is that possible?' Sam asked. 'Those hand controls –'

'Oh, believe it,' Rem said.

* * *

Sam decided we should go back to my place, which was closest, so

Rem could make some calls. 'Keys, please,' I said to Sam.

Rem rode in the front with me. Sam and Michele rode in the bed with their backs to us, bracing the wheelchair between them. I had the feeling this was illegal, but not for me. Rem, meanwhile, hauled himself up pretty easily. In the restaurant I had pointed out the exact time he had discovered his car was gone, and he had thanked me and noted it down on the back of the bill. Now we were all going to my place.

Back at the house I had crackers and a bottle, or eggs for omelettes, depending on which way the party went.

My street was very quiet, like an audience is quiet, as we got down from my truck. Michele got down fast, smiling. Sam stayed on the bed to help me get the wheelchair down. It scraped a little, making both Rem and me wince. I would like to be able to say that we laid a good piece of plywood over the front steps to make a decent ramp, but there was no plywood or anything useful. So Rem worked himself up backwards, step by step, while Sam and I carried the wheelchair. We only snagged it once, on the doorstep. The night smelled of woodsmoke, and I was taking deep breaths.

The phone was in the kitchen. I gave Rem a pen and pad. I had been a technical writer, and had a lot of pads. 'What is this number?' Rem asked, pointing at my phone.

I had been a technical writer with a PR firm. I wrote press releases, brochures, and manuals, accumulating pockets of expertise like so many core samples. I had had my own office. Sometimes I fell asleep at my desk. I quit, citing personal reasons, even though I didn't really have any. At the office they assumed someone I loved had died and were nicer to me than I deserved. On my last day I lifted a lot of stationery supplies, mostly coloured pads and ballpoints.

Thinking of these things, I wrote my phone number at the top of Rem's green pad and went into the living room.

Sam and Michele had put themselves in my big stuffed chairs. They were both slumped down, with legs spread and hands gripping the armrests, as though bracing for G-forces. 'Music!' Sam said, and they laughed. He started conducting from his chair, tossing his head and cueing the furniture. He is so blond his eyebrows are white and his eyelashes invisible. Aging will not look so bad on him.

'You're fired!' he shouted at my bookcase. Michele was giggling in waves, like a baby. Although she would stop periodically, you could tell she couldn't break out of the rhythm of it.

I put some band music on the radio. After a while they settled down and we started to talk. At some point I equipped each of us with a Scotch in a mug. In fact I had liquor glasses, but I liked the mugs better. Michele seemed to lap at hers, as though her tongue were a sponge and she could get to the bottom of her drink by absorption. She said little but kept smiling at Sam, at me.

Rem stuck his head around the door. 'Hey hey hey!' I said.

'So that was you.' He took in the room, the pleasant soft music, the three of us chatting. 'Facilities?' he asked.

This evening is just not ending for you, is it, I thought. I showed him where to go.

When he came back I thought they would all get up and leave, but Rem parked himself in our circle and when Sam offered him a drink – Sam had the bottle just then – he accepted.

'Make all your calls?' I asked. The Scotch had screwed me down into a little box, where I was steady and could see straight so long as I didn't move. I felt fine.

Sam and Michele were dancing. She had a hand on the back of his neck, and he had a hand on the small of her back to keep their hips pressed together; and Rem and I watched, invisible.

After that she insisted on dancing with me, probably trying to erase what she had just done with my friend Sam. Then she went after Rem, the way she had gone after him to eat her seafood. She pulled on his arms and swayed her hips, trying to get him to dance in his chair. Finally he did some rhythmic things with his shoulders and head, and she copied him, holding his hands, both of them smiling. So that was something they did. It lasted for about a minute.

'Okay,' Rem said. Then it was time for them to go. Sam said he could walk, he could walk, and left right away. Michele called a yellow cab and Rem called a special cab. The special cab would bring a ramp for my stairs. The yellow cab came first. 'Got all your monkeys and parrots?' I asked her at the door.

After she was gone, Rem started fiddling around in his chair. It was awkward to watch. I noticed he kept valuables tucked behind him – wallet, water bottle. He twisted away from me now, checking his stuff, getting ready to go. I was glad he was leaving. I didn't like him.

'I'd like to catch some more of your games,' I said. 'Got a schedule, there, somewhere?'

'Call the parish,' he said.

'I guess the Catholic Church has been pretty good to you guys,' I said. A van with a plank strapped to the roofrack pulled up in front of my house. When the driver opened his door, a yellow light went on inside. Rem raised a hand to the driver, bumped himself over the doorstep, and pulled my door closed behind him.

The phone was ringing, I realized after a while.

An angry person informed me that my car had not been stolen, it had been towed. The person had not started out angry, but I was having trouble hearing the individual words. I stared at the green pad with my phone number and several other phone numbers squared up beneath it. 'ATLANTIC,' Rem had underlined next to one of them.

'You have to display your handicapped permit in a handicapped zone or your vehicle will be impounded, Mr Vandervelden,' the person was saying. 'We've been through this. Now, you will need this number –'

I hung up and got my bank book from a desk drawer. I had six thousand dollars left, plus the truck, plus a few bills in my wallet – enough that I could buy breakfast tomorrow morning and not have to crack the six thousand. Everything else was television.

RUN

Every time the bus started to move, the driver turned off the fluorescent lights. Then the inside of the bus was the same colour as the outside, but warmer. It pulled from block to block, dragging the city, heading for the last run when it could stop and everyone would go.

The girl reached a couple of fingers into the inside pocket of her jacket and fingered a bus ticket, a quarter, a tampon. An inch of paper, a metal disc, a cotton bullet – that was how she had been thinking about things lately. It was later than late and she was on her way home.

'Honey?' the fat man said. 'Is that you?'

She had not seen him get on.

The fat man sat down next to her, sealing her against the window. He had scars on his chin which were almost invisible because of his fatness. The scars came from a can opener. He received them in his youth, he had said, but that was past. Now he was fat and gentle and not really to be feared. She had stayed awake all the first night, just in case, but there had been no need. A week later – bored, nervous – she had left.

'Where are you living now?' he asked.

For the past month she had lived with two other people on the top floor of a hundred-year-old house. The girl had crucifixes tattooed on the soles of her feet and a yellow cat. The boy was a gardener and smelled of sweat and pine trees. They were strangers and the house was their shell.

'How are the fish?' she asked. The fat man kept black mollies.

'Pining for you.'

She remembered him feeding them food dust from a shaker. After he fed them he would tip his head back and tap some into his own mouth. Once she asked him what it was like.

'Tangy,' he said.

She had left home when she felt she would always be capable of securing for herself milk and warm bread, and sometimes coffee and apples. She had bought a flute, deep downtown, in a toy shop slipped between a sex boutique and the fluttering glow of an arcade. The flute squirted a clear tone like a small brown bird. She had sat cross-legged on the pavement like a girl Buddha under the ball lights of a marquee, holding the toy flute in her fingertips. That was where the fat man found her. Later when he became troublesome she bought a brown paper envelope in a shop that sold things for skin. Inside the envelope was a smaller plastic bag and inside the plastic bag was black powder. She washed her hair with the powder and it left a dirty wet rinse around the sink and when she flipped her head back to confront the mirror she looked pale and milky-sweet with her new dark hair. But he had found her anyway, just stepped on a bus and found her. She realized she had been foolish to suppose she could evade a fat man's love just by changing her colours.

She reached up and pulled the cord. A light went on in the front of the bus.

'Excuse me, please,' she said to the fat man.

He moved his knees sideways to let her past but caught her hand, his fat thumb in her palm. She looked down at him.

'Is it you?' he said.

He let her go. The bus stopped. She stepped down and out. The driver turned off the lights as the bus started up.

The fat man got off at the next stop. By the time he caught sight of her again she was just disappearing into a dark house in the soft warm malign heart of the metropolis. He waited for a light to go on in a window but no light came on. He noted the address with a tiny pencil in a tiny notebook he carried in his wallet, before turning back the way he'd come.

* * *

The next night, the Crucifix Girl took a pill and lost her mind.

'It's all in the wrist,' she kept saying. She spiralled around the room, popping off the walls like a bumper car. 'Don't look at *me*,' she said.

The boy gestured silently to the girl. They went into another room where the boy had a mattress and a desk lamp on the floor.

He closed the door. The girl knelt and clicked on the lamp. It spilled an ancient mellow light.

The boy wore his wrist in a bandage wrapped to the stiffness of plaster. He had wrenched something in it the day before in dealing with a fractious azalea. Soon he would learn not to go pulling on nature, but he had not learned it yet. All that day he had sat in the upstairs room looking at his hand, turning it over, wanting to scratch, waiting for something to happen.

'What's your name?' he asked.

'Ernestine,' she said, taking off her T-shirt.

He raised his eyebrows. 'Ernestine's a black girl's name.'

'So?'

'So nothing,' he said. 'Come here.'

Later they heard shouting beneath the window. They got up. The boy put his back to the wall and pulled the curtain back slightly with his good hand, letting the streetlight slice his face. He took a quick look and then he looked at the girl. He raised his eyebrows in a way she was beginning to recognize.

'Honey,' the fat man called again.

The girl looked around for something to put on. She began to dress in a mixture of their clothing. She felt this to be a kind of arrogance but the pain up inside made her feel entitled.

'Maybe he'll go away,' the boy said. He held the bandaged hand lightly against his chest.

She belted her jeans. 'No,' she said. 'Not him.'

* * *

The fat man let the girl lead him upstairs to a big peeling room with an iron chandelier, where she invited him to sit on a box. She sat opposite, low to the floor in an old armchair. She sat up straight with her legs tucked demurely to one side and crossed at the ankles, as though she were conducting an interview. She wore her jeans and a red flannel shirt he had not seen before which was too big for her. A boy came bare-chested from an adjoining room and stood behind her. He saw they were both barefoot. The boy never took his eyes off the fat man but reached down to touch her shoulder as she sat and let his hand stay there. She reached up for it and then the fat man understood.

'Oh, go put your clothes on,' he said to the boy. 'I'm not here for a cockfight.'

They said nothing.

'I came to see if you were happy,' he said.

She straightened her back. 'Oh, I'm happy,' she said.

She was not malicious, he thought, only a child; but she could not hope to sustain a child's life if she stayed much longer on her own. He glanced around the room, at the blue mould skimming down from the ceiling making the walls look as though they were hung with velour, the punched-in window, the unlit white candles on the bare floor, the Crucifix Girl twisting and twitching in a kind of sleep on the couch.

'It's not so warm here,' he said.

She said nothing.

'I bought you a blanket,' he said.

'You bought a blanket.'

'Come home.'

He saw the boy gently work his fingers into the hair at the nape of her neck. He saw her lean her head back slightly, into his hand. He reckoned between the two of them they had had less sex than Christmases. It was the age for tragedy. 'Come home.'

The boy cleared his throat. He appeared to be choosing his words carefully.

'Who is this guy?' he said.

'He gave me a room.'

He held up a thick hand and counted off his fingers. 'Room. Board. Books. Hand cream. Gave is the operative word. Did I ask for money?'

'I paid,' she said. 'Didn't you find it? I left everything I had in the blue bowl.'

A small rice-bowl of buzzing cobalt. She had left it on the windowsill filled with small bills, coins, a piece of amber. He had not disarranged it except to move it from the windowsill to the mantel where it would not be disturbed when he aired her room. He had not touched the contents. That was her business, when she came back.

'You liked that bowl.'

'It was a handsome bowl.'

'I want you to have it.'

'I don't want the bowl.'

'But I want you to have it.'

'Look,' the boy said. 'You're not by any chance her father?'

'Well,' he said. 'You could think of me that way if you like. That is, technically no, but all the emotions are there. I think that counts for a lot.'

'He's not my father,' she said.

The fat man considered the room again.

'You know, I would not desire to be in this place in a fire,' he said.

'What fire?' the boy said.

The girl cleared her throat.

'Look,' the boy said. 'What if we drive you home now. You must be tired.'

The fat man looked at the girl.

'You came all this way,' she said. 'We could do that.'

He looked at her.

'You could do that,' he said finally. 'That could be a start.'

* * *

The boy and the girl went into the boy's room to put on their shoes. The boy looked at the bed. It was a mess.

'I'll look after you,' he said.

She wore black boots which took elaborate lacing and she knelt by the window for the green milk of the streetlight. She took the end of a long lace in her teeth and held it taut while she fiddled with the boot. The fat man appeared in the doorway.

'Just making sure you aren't getting distracted,' he said. 'I know youth can be distractable.'

* * *

The boy drove an ailing Malibu with tartan tail-lights and a floor bleak with crud. The girl sat next to him and the man who was not her father sat in the back seat. It was black dark and the fat man in the back was a rich voice and nothing more.

'It's good of you to do this for me,' he said.

'No, no,' the boy said. He was driving carefully, with much attention to lights and yield signs and speed limits and various other cautions that flared at him out of the darkness. He did not want to be stopped.

'It's a long way.'

'It's the least we can do.'

The fat man gave that some thought. 'Yes,' he said.

They drove for a while.

'Look at you,' the fat man said to the boy. 'You've got a girl and a car. Your life is jam. Are you aware of that?'

The boy thought, jam.

The girl and the fat man began to talk about the girl's hair. The fat man was chiding her but she was making him laugh. He listened to them laugh, his girl and the fat man. He didn't know what they were talking about. He couldn't see anything wrong with his girl's hair. He couldn't see what there was to laugh about. But he was supposed to be helping her out and here she was getting festive.

The fat man began to tell a story with his voice.

'I knew a girl,' he said. 'You could drain gold and riches onto her until she didn't know where to look. But was she grateful?'

'Was she?' the girl said.

'She ran,' he said. 'Then she shaved her arms and got herself a little tan and figured she was ready for the world. She even got herself a cub with a hurt paw. What do you make of that?'

'Soft,' she said. 'Very soft.'

The boy eased the car up to a red light.

'I know a girl who ran,' the fat man said dreamily. 'But where is she now? Why does she think she can hide from me?'

She said nothing. Gingerly, the boy raised his cast-hand to lay it across her shoulders, to remind her who was who. The hand lay there, throbbing.

'Pets can be fun,' the fat man said. 'Don't think I don't know it.'

The light turned green. The boy took his hand back to drive. For a while no one spoke. Suddenly the boy said, 'I feel like a doughnut.'

The girl seemed not to have heard so he appealed to the fat man. 'A doughnut, you know?' he said. 'What do you say?'

She was angry all of a sudden. She was looking out the window but he felt it in the way she held her head.

'Son,' the fat man said sadly, 'I can always manage a bite.'

'Pull in here,' the girl said. They were coming up to a gas station. 'I have to use the toilet.'

He pulled into a parking lot and she jumped out. They watched her run to the white-lit pantry and come out with the key. She disappeared around the side of the building.

While they waited the fat man talked. He talked about how he had painted her room blue after she left, as though it had always been her room, and how he kept a bowl of pink speckled apples for her on the table under the window. He talked about dawn through the yellow kitchen curtains and the world of trash and sorrow she faced beyond them. He talked like someone who had waited a long time for a dark car and a courteous stranger.

The boy didn't want to talk to the fat man about the girl. He concentrated on reading all the signs around the gas station. Milk, cigarettes, soft cloth wash, regular, super, supreme.

She was gone a long time.

'She's angry now,' the fat man said. 'You've made her angry.'

'Why?' the boy asked.

'She won't eat with people watching,' the fat man said. 'She gets anxious.' He shook his head and looked flat at the boy. Then he thrust his arm out into the front seat. 'Feel that,' he said. 'Go on, touch it. That's flesh. It's nothing to be afraid of.'

'No,' the boy said. 'I know.'

'Touch it, though,' the fat man said. 'Go on. You're not afraid of me? Me and my big messy heart?'

The boy prodded the arm with a finger, like he was buying chicken.

'That's it,' the fat man said.

They watched through the windshield as the girl came back across the parking lot.

'Oh yes,' the fat man said. 'I could tell you some things about Stella.'

'Who?'

She opened the door and got in, swirling the air in the car with a sweet chill, a little piece of the night. 'Miss me?' she asked.

'Who?' the boy said.

* * *

In the doughnut shop the boy and the girl took a booth while the fat man went up to the counter to choose. He chose multi-sprinkles for the boy and French for himself and the girl. He liked the delicacy of a French doughnut, how it was crisper on the outside and softer than a plain cake doughnut, and how it broke into regular pieces along the ridges.

He watched the girl break her doughnut open and pick out the fluffy white inside, leaving it in flocks on the plate.

'I think you'd do better to come with me,' the fat man said quietly. 'I really do.'

Under the table, the boy put his hand over the girl's hand. He cleared his throat.

'You hush,' the fat man said. 'Right now I'm talking to her.'

For the next few minutes the boy listened as the girl and the fat man discussed the past and the future. His head felt like a water balloon, full of thoughts too heavy to be contained for long behind the thin skin of his face. He felt them rolling around darkly and the fat man's voice like a gushing faucet pressuring him. Then he felt the girl dig her nails into his hand under the table. She was saying something about using the bathroom.

'Again?' the fat man said.

'For crying out loud,' the boy said. 'If she has to go, she has to go.'

He felt her hand slip from his as she stood up. 'Yes,' she said. 'And if I want to jump out the window, I'll do that too.'

'I take an interest, that's all,' the fat man said.

They watched her walk up to the counter with the glass-fronted pastry case and the cash register and the bottles of juice, jewel-coloured. They watched the doughnut boy open the little gate in the counter and let her through and into the back where the toilet would be.

'For that matter, I think I have to go too,' the boy said. 'You have a problem with that?'

'You are not my concern here,' the fat man said.

He watched the boy walk up to the counter and disappear after the girl.

'Come back,' he said.

* * *

He found her sitting outside, leaning against the back wall of the doughnut shop. It was dark back there and her face was smudged by the darkness.

'I wasn't sure you'd make it,' she said. 'I waited twenty minutes at the gas station.'

'I'm here now,' the boy said.

'We should go,' she said. 'Before he comes looking. Too bad the car's right out front.'

'Even if he sees us,' the boy said, taking her hands and pulling her to her feet. 'Then what? He won't chase us. He can't run.'

'I don't want him to see us,' the girl said. 'Let's just please get out of here. You got your keys?'

'Who's Stella?' he asked.

'Who do you think?'

They walked round to the front of the building. They walked straight to the car and got in and drove away.

'We can't go back to the house,' she said after a minute. Cars passed them regularly, like exhalations.

'That's all right,' the boy said. 'I know some places.'

'We haven't done anything wrong. We took him partway,' she said.

'That's right,' the boy said. He was driving fast.

Ten minutes later he pulled the car over. They got out at the side of the highway. The boy opened the hood and looked inside. She came and stood beside him. Together they looked inside.

'What's wrong?' she asked.

Nothing, but he wouldn't tell her that yet. 'I don't know.'

'Where are we?'

'I don't know.'

'Now what?'

'Look,' the boy said. 'Listen. I don't know. I do not know. Maybe the fat man would know.'

'Sure he would,' she said. 'He's got the world sewn up so tight you can't turn around. Forget it.' She yawned, turning away.

When he saw she had got in the back and not the front he kicked some dirt with his toe and started to smile.

They slept in a tangle on the back seat of the Malibu. By morning, stiff with cold, they resembled something which could be picked up with spaghetti claws, trailing legs and hair.

* * *

The fat man worked his finger down through a hole in the red vinyl seat, into the foam, and wiggled it. Pretty soon he figured it out. He felt no sudden pain, the free fall of treachery. It was just that one moment he was waiting for them to come back from the toilet and the next moment he was some fat man in a booth eating a doughnut and drinking coffee and worrying the upholstery. He knew quickly and blandly, like figures in sand blown over by wind. Here, gone. It was an easy thing to know.

He decided to give them a good start since, as the adult in the situation, he felt he had the advantage. He drank his coffee to the dregs and then he drank them too. He rolled the pithy grit against the roof of his mouth with his tongue. Dregs were only bitter when you were not really paying attention. As he explored the texture of them, the taste shifted from bitterness to another taste, one he could not judge with emotions. It was just a taste.

He set the coffee cup on his empty plate and pushed it away. He ate the girl's doughnut and what was left of the boy's doughnut. He wiped the rim of each of their mugs with his thumb and drank their coffees, the boy's sweet and blond with cream, the girl's black and sweet.

He rose and went to the counter and asked the doughnut boy to change a dollar for him so he could use the phone but the doughnut boy reached under the counter and pulled out a phone and set it on the counter, straining its lead, and said there was no charge. The doughnut boy had acne and freckles and had not liked the sight of the boy walking after the girl any more than the fat man. He had not liked that business of the back doors. Therefore he pulled a phone book from under the counter and helped the fat man find a cab.

* * *

Two hours later, a devastated room service trolley sat by the door, waiting to be taken away and spiffed up for breakfast. The fat man lay on his back on the hotel bed and stared at the ceiling. He had just eaten and now he was resting.

He had intended to return to the hundred-year-old house but in the cab fatigue hit him like a tide of honey. He decided to treat himself to a night of rest and told the driver to take him to a nice hotel. At the hotel he asked for a nice room. The woman at the desk took his credit card and passed it through her computer and typed something. The computer zipped and printed. She tore off the slip and smiled and handed back his credit card and a pen to sign the slip. He liked the way she handed him the pen. She was not afraid of his hand touching hers in passing, as many women were. She handed him a plastic card with the hotel's name on it and called it a key and said she had given him the nicest room of all.

The room turned out to be a quilted box of floral tapestry and pink light and nylon curtains, fireproof but meant to look gauzy, and a four-poster bed with crimson bows and sashes, and an enormous gilt mirror. It was the honeymoon suite. The fat man found that by draping his coat over the mirror he could obscure himself above the knee, but after that he was stuck with what there was.

The room service menu lay on the faux-oak panelled TV. The fat man ordered immediately. He ordered clear soup and steak au poivre and chipped potatoes with gravy and a whole wheat roll and a sourdough roll and baby carrots with mint and garlic jelly and mineral water and lime sorbet and blueberry cheesecake and coffee. After he hung up he checked out the mini bar. He fixed himself a Scotch and water, and opened a package of salted airplane peanuts with a pair of nail-clippers from the bathroom. He went back to the mini bar and found an ice cube, plopped it in his Scotch and sucked the splash off his fingers. He phoned room service again and added a small winter salad. He hung up and turned on the TV. He watched cliff diving from Acapulco and a news item about car theft. Then a boy knocked and called 'Room service,' and he turned off the TV.

On his way to the door, the fat man took a box of matches from the glass ashtray on the TV and dropped them into his pocket so he would not forget them in the morning. Rags he would need too, and gasoline. He did not think she would go backwards, but he would tend to the hundred-year-old house just in case. He would char that option, forcing her on towards him. His love was that grand.

* * *

The boy woke first. Cold, he rubbed the girl's back until she began to shift. When she was awake he said what was on his mind.

'Eggs, bacon, juice, toast, coffee,' he said. 'Pancakes.'

The girl sat up and shook her hair down out of her eyes. She rubbed her face with the wrist of the boy's red shirt, which she was still wearing from the night before. She stretched.

'Grapefruit?' the boy said.

She smiled and pushed her palms against the roof of the car.

He hugged her, then reached across and opened the door. They braved the morning.

Outside it was clean cold and early and a few cars were rocketing by in mad whispers and curls of mist. The girl said maybe they could hitch a ride but the boy said he had to do something first. He glanced around and then climbed down the embankment at the side of the highway until he was in a field of weeds below the level of the cars, where he unzipped and pissed on the sedge. Hunger was flexing and crawling inside him. He zipped up and tightened his belt a notch and slapped his pockets with his good hand for his keys. He guessed they must have fallen out in the night because his pockets were empty. But when he scrambled back up the embankment and onto the gravel shoulder of the highway the car was gone and the girl was gone and he never saw her again, although he spent many weeks searching.

TRIALS

I want that one over there, with the spidery black bikini and the ball peen husband. She wouldn't let me down.

A liquorice-gummed husky is paws-up to the drinking fountain, tonguing the water arc, scaring the little thirsty children who stand well back, pointing and cringing as at a bully in a hair suit, this hot day at the beach.

Back at the apartment, we had the sashes up and a breeze was nosing through, bothering the plants and the blue flames under the coffee water. She was packing again, although this time it seemed to mean something. You know the kind of apartment I mean – hardwood floors, garlic on the counter, candles in the bathroom, brown paint peeling off something – our first apartment together. So what.

'Hey?' she says.

This is her way of asking for help. She doesn't say what she wants, she emits this – utterance. I want to hit her. Instead, I hold the box flaps while she tapes them flat. 'You don't have to go,' I say.

'You don't have to stay, either,' she says. 'I'm managing, here. Why don't you go out for a while? I'll probably still be here when you get back.'

This is either sexiness or tragedy. Which? She blinks her eyes at me. Glasses and ponytail, white T-shirt, white winter legs in red shorts on this first hot day of the year. I'm supposed to know? 'OK, bye,' I say.

The crying's been done for days, thank God.

At the beach, I stake my claim under a shade tree and watch the bodies. The one I would choose for myself arrives. I read the words on her T-shirt before she strips it, 'Property of Vale First Baptist', and my heart turns on like a light.

The girl who's currently leaving me is a social worker. She calls this a trial separation. I am amused. When we found the place she called our first few months a trial period. I found out she'd try any-thing. I pun, I do.

Her clients phone her at home, with the slow voices of the afflicted; and she is patient with them, in her falsely patient voice. I have to listen to this, in the evenings, in my own home. I deserve better.

That man over there has what I deserve. I don't mean the crew-cut, the mirrored shades, the tree-trunk demeanour, but the wife or whatever she is, the prettiness on the blanket, who would right now appear to be looking at me. I would call her look curious, alert. I would call it something new.

My social worker says next to me, she is sane and solid. She means she's a prize, but she isn't. She has a hundred flaws. Her glasses are too big for her face. She sings well-badly, with a lilt and a catch, like a country singer. She thinks she's smarter than I am because she's smarter than her clients. Then when we're watching the news she'll wake up two minutes into a segment and say, 'What was that gun? A Glock?' The next day she'll refer casually, in conversation, to a Glock.

She kisses too much during sex and I don't like it.

She calls me austere. She says I get angry when people and events don't line up tall and tidy, like spaghetti jars. When she gets nervous her voice goes small and she follows me around the apartment, agreeing with me. When she feels good she criticizes and listens to herself talk. 'Shut up, you cow,' I say, and she grins ruefully. Why? is what I want to know.

My job is computers, is systems, is trouble-shooting for a firm of sixty lawyers. I don't understand their work and they don't understand mine, but we drink the same coffee. We've got a nice little ecosystem going. Girlfriend's job is the salt mines, granted – terrible, suffering people are her people – and then she comes home to an asshole like me. Last week she's telling me a horror story starring some deranged, abused frog she calls Mr Malone, and I pick up the phone to order pizza.

'Are you even listening to me?' she says.

'Somewhat.'

'Forget it,' she says, and I thank her. It's that she gets querulous when she gets angry, loud and querulous and earnest and dim. Between pizza ordering and pizza coming she tells me she's had enough of me and has arranged to move in with a girlfriend for a while. Sure, I'm guilty and bad as the dark side of the moon. My soul is a pocked wasteland, yes, yes, OK.

So I try to remember what she was telling me about Frog Malone. I trickle blond sand through my fingers and try to think. But my pretty Baptist is on her feet, if you please, coming towards me with a wicker basket on her arm. Trippingly she comes, and I look at the basket and think hopefully: strawberries?

'Hi there!' she says.

She kneels beside me and flips open the top of her little hamper. Inside are rows of baby jars. She takes one out to show me. It's filled with a thick blue substance, which seems OK to me, seems normal, because her nearness is messing me up. It's nice.

'You rub it in like so,' she's saying. She's got the cap off one of these babies, is rubbing a finger of blue into her pale arm. 'Totally, totally natural,' she's saying. Her arm is turning blue.

I'm nodding, mesmerized. Above me, the tree is whispering. 'It's only money,' the leaves are saying, crossing and uncrossing one another like scissors, occasionally shearing and releasing one of their own.

'Did you make this?' I ask her.

'In my kitchen.'

I hold out my arm and she says, 'Five dollars.' I give her money and she leaves me the open jar. 'I would recommend using it within forty-eight hours,' she says.

'Help me,' I say, holding out my arm again.

'Also you can eat it,' she says, backing away. 'I don't know why you'd want to, but I mean, it's that harmless.'

'It's one hell of a product,' calls the husband. He's under the next tree with his shirt off, selling to the trail-bike girls with the husky, but he's keeping an eye on me. I must have an off look.

'Divide and conquer, hey?' I say to her, nodding at the husband. I mean to say I see their strategy – she takes the men, he takes the women – and am not conned. I am, though. 'Hey?' I say, but she's moved on.

I think about going back to the apartment and rubbing the girlfriend's white legs blue with this stuff, and making her tell me about Frog Malone getting his head stomped, whatever, and making myself listen. I think about holding hands, and hugging and kissing and whatever she wants. 'Oh God, don't go,' she would want me to say. We could cry a little, together. That would right our little cup. It has in the past.

Meanwhile, I eat the sunscreen. I know my social worker isn't going anywhere, and anyway I think it's interesting to find new uses for a thing, once you've paid for it and you know it's yours.

EVERY LITTLE THING

'Imposing pissant, isn't he,' John says of our professor. He's trying to cheer me up.

Fat apricot koi are sharking and shimmying in the fake lake. Our great bearded professor this morning wore a shirt the colour of these koi. He stands straight, though, unlike these trees – twisted, clever, *listening*.

Across the water is a tea-house, low and jolly and warm as a paper lantern. When I was a child I would have intended to live there with food and books, stone silent while the caretaker locked the garden door. Now I just want to sleep in it, pray and sleep.

We're in medical school together, John and I – first year. He's rifling my knapsack. My anatomy binder is in there, Day-Timer, Lypsyl, pens, wads of case studies I'm supposed to have read. He pulls out *Imitation of Christ*. 'I love you, Gwen, but you're very pretentious,' he says.

This Japanese garden is at the bottom of campus, in the heart of an inky cedar forest, down towards the sea. The faculty of medicine is on higher ground, jewel in a crown of parking lots. I bring John here to give the other first-years a break from his mouth. People assume that because he can't help himself, he's not very astute. They're wrong.

He's standing now, kicking at the park bench I'm sitting on. 'Stupid bench!' he shouts, and laughs. I offer him some of my sandwich. 'Cheese is evil,' he says, and eats it. He kicks the bench again.

'Ssh,' I say. 'This is a quiet garden.'

'Well, until I got here, right.' Now he squats in front of me and pats my head. 'Cheer up, Gwen,' he says. He has thick hair and tiny eyes. 'I don't actually remember what you're upset about, but I know it was important.'

It was, but I say, 'Ah, no.'

It starts to rain in long staining threads.

* * *

Hearts and flowers. As for the future, I'm thinking surgery. I have no problem with cooking and sewing, and surgery seems to involve significant elements of cooking and sewing. As for the future, I'm thinking marriage and all the ancient ways – home and hearth, church, civic duty, family – filling in those blanks. It's a plan. I say to myself, Gwen, abide by this solid plan.

The campus Ecumenical Centre *is* cosy. It *is* a warm and yellow place when the world is cold and blue. It *is* a harbour and a sanctuary, smelling sweetly of bake sales past. I used to come here for choir until I quit choir. I used to come here to watch TV until I got sick of dorm girls in sleeping bags watching *The Lion King* on the VCR.

I have an appointment to see my pastor, Pastor Kyle. My parents are Anglicans up where the air is so thin you don't talk about it, but I'm trying out the Baptists. Baptists talk about it. Today I have questions about the Council of Nicaea.

'Have I signed you up for the car wash?' Pastor Kyle asks. He keeps a messy office, paper on the floor, with ugly accessories – rainbow penholder, bulbous IKEA lamp, photograph of his girlfriend who is on a mission in Mexico. Also he's growing a goatee. I tell him I'm tired all the time. I start to cry. I tell him I'm just tired out and I hate every little thing in his piece-of-shit office.

He suggests Health Services. 'Med school is hard work,' he says. 'Do you think stress is getting to you?'

I stand up and look around. I'm not done crying but I'll have to finish it in the bathroom.

'About that other thing,' he says. 'The real scholar around here is Father Rennie. I'll bet he has some literature. Sit down, Gwen.'

'That's all right,' I say.

'No, it isn't,' he says. 'Sit down.'

When I finally leave he recommends Health Services, prayer, and regular swimming. 'Imagine you belong to someone else,' he says. 'Which you do. Don't punish what isn't yours.'

* * *

'I'd like to thank everyone for their tolerance today,' the bus driver says through the microphone.

Another rank, dank day, pitchy already at four-thirty. John has been talking politics – loudly – talking political correctness, special interest groups, special privileges, the economy, welfare. 'The Maritimes, that farce!' he says.

I try to shush him. 'I can't, Gwen,' he says reasonably. I know he can't. 'These people should read Marcuse – THE INTOLERANCE OF TOLERANCE.' He yells that last bit, for the driver.

'Shut up, mate,' someone says.

'Who said that?' John demands. 'I'll butter the walls with you!' He's grinning.

'Bye, now,' I say. It's my stop, or close enough.

'OK, I'll call you, Gwen,' he calls after me. 'We have a lot to talk about!'

Now John, you would think, paediatrician. With that manic energy, you would think, Doctor John, good guy, makes you laugh. Except, no, Doctor John is thinking epidemiology – research. He broke his baby cousin by accident, playing with her. He stepped on her foot and now she has a permanent limp.

'When was this?' I asked when he told me.

'When was this. Last year.'

I have a basement suite near the university, near the empty, washed beaches. Most of the houses in my neighbourhood are massive warrens of student rooms. Their windows at night have the appeal of firelight and spaghetti suppers, October leaves, bed. I have two big rooms, big bunkers, and a lot of locks on the door. I don't mind living like in a cave.

Experience tells me I will have half an hour's peace. I make strong black tea and flip through the Bible. Isaiah: *Behold, I have refined thee, but not with silver; I have chosen thee in the furnace of affliction.*

At five forty the phone starts to ring.

At five forty-seven it stops. I put the kettle on, pull out my binder, and start to read.

At six fifteen, John is at my door. 'I knew you were home, just not answering,' he says. He's breathing hard, blinking. Rain is dripping off his hair and ears. I hand him his tea. He slurps at it, pants, grinning and nodding. 'Oh, my tongue,' he says. 'I can always tell.'

I take his coat and hang it up. I look at his shoes and he takes them off. I go to the stove and start building sandwiches while oil heats and thins in the frying pan.

'Poor Gwen,' John says. He runs a fingertip along the top of a doorframe, looking for dust. He cranes over the sink, looking for grot in the drain. With a crepe flipper I offer him a fried cheese sandwich. 'You eat a lot of cheese,' he says, but he takes it. He eats it pacing up and down, wiping his mouth on his wrist. I sit in my big chair while he talks and talks. The nice thing about John, I don't have to listen. I can sit and think my own grey thoughts. I can be myself.

He stops and looks at my books on Zen. I have a shelf of Zen. 'How many religions have you *been*?' he asks.

'Just the two.'

'Did you shave your head?'

'You're thinking of Tibetan Buddhists,' I say.

'That wasn't you?'

'Wasn't me.'

'What did you do?'

I straighten up. '*Zazen*. Five a.m. meditation.'

'See.' He leans forward excitedly, like he's on to me. 'You have the Calvinist temperament. Why are you with folks who eat cookies for Jesus?'

'They let me sleep in.'

John shakes his head. 'Sleep is important, I know it. Still, I don't like it when you're not serious with me. Say.'

'What?'

'Can I brush my teeth?' He bumps off my desk. 'Ow. Gwen?'

'Carefully,' I say.

While he brushes his teeth I wash up. 'Scrubbing the rainbows from her teaspoons,' he says, emerging. 'Swab them counters, Gwendolyn. Your bathroom will get you to heaven.'

He makes cleanliness sound like the loneliest of perversions. I say, 'Time to go home, now.'

After he's gone, I straighten everything he's bumped or kicked or picked up and put down wrong. I wash in cold water and drink a glass of cold water and go to bed. It's early still, but I've reached the end of the useful day and – decision taken – I'm desperate to go under.

* * *

The next day I get to my first class ten minutes late. There's nothing much to slow me down in the morning – I don't, for instance, use cosmetics or braid my hair or eat breakfast. It's true, I prefer a minimalist kick – the cheese and cold water and one pair of shoes, like that – testing my self-discipline and trying to purify my thinking. Some days I get confused. *Where are you going!* on the Korean church at Renfrew. Or the veterans' memorial on Hastings: *Is it nothing to you!* The lateness is so I don't have to sit with John.

'Question right here!' he calls, waving both arms and making grasping motions with his hands, like he's pulling in affection. He does this several time a lecture, five lectures a day. He's appalling. 'Hi, Gwen!' he adds. I smile minimally and go to the back of the theatre.

'This question and one more,' the koi professor is saying. 'That's your ration for today.'

'He's a prick,' John says later. 'I annoy him on purpose.'

From a different bench, a different perspective: the lake obscured by a glitter of leaves. John is walking on the wrong side of the low croquet hoop fencing separating the path from the moss. 'No, John,' I say.

'Oh, fucking *anal*,' he says. 'The straight and narrow road to *hell*. Hellions and scallions.'

'Don't come over tonight, OK?' I say. 'I have work to do.'

He shrugs.

* * *

Backstroking, I mash my head. I haul out sniffling and go to the showers, silver jets and beads, to sluice off the chlorine. In the change room I dab at my head with a bunched towel, blot my face. I haven't been swimming in years. My body is weak as shadow, trembling convulsively like the water shadow on the ceiling of the aquatic complex, a hundred feet up, the moment before I hit the wall.

105

The doctor at Health Services wants a red blood cell count. He wants me to attend a meeting on eating awareness.

'Maybe if I tried vitamins,' I say. 'For the tiredness.'

'There are four food groups,' he says, holding up four fingers. 'Four! Explore them! Why am I telling you this? You're a medical student!'

'I have this tiredness. I have dizziness, crying, insomnia, trouble concentrating. I have this friend –'

'Grilled breast of chicken,' he says. 'A little rice, a little salad, big thick milkshake. Take the night off. Get your friend to take you to a movie. Eat and relax. Swim on your front. You'll be fine.'

'What?'

'You heard me,' he says. 'Next.'

* * *

The next time I see John he's got a cast on the right arm, elbow to knuckle, fingers curled. 'Come on and ask me,' he says.

He follows me down through the garden door. The sky has gone light and dangerous with snow. A glassy crust encroaches on the lake. Frost has a lock on the world; the bamboo spears are tipped with it. The ground is hard, the trees brittle, like etchings of trees. Exams are coming.

'Look,' I say, a little louder than I should, and then stop. I need to get rid of him. He's a torment and a distraction. Sure, it's a sexy sickness as sicknesses go, but I've done my bit of charity – of love – and now I want my rest. 'Look,' I say.

'I see it.'

A spike of dry lightning, another, pink in the queer light of the failing year. Another strolling couple on the curved stone bridge turns around to look. 'What happened?' one of them asks.

'I fell,' John says. 'How much do you want to know?' When the couple has passed he says, 'I hate it here. This garden is just the idea of a garden. It's not a sanctuary, it's an excuse. You think I can't read your mind?'

After he's gone, I open up my lunch – a Styrofoam hutch of beef-broccoli special from Japan Noodle Factory – tangle the sauce into my noodles with a cheap fork, and bundle it up to my mouth. It's good, warm food, gently steaming in the cold air. The broccoli is green as paint.

* * *

After exams, I go home for Christmas. My dad and I take a walk in the woods by the reservoir.

'I remember when you were a little girl,' he says. 'You were never happy. Nothing was ever good enough for you. Nothing was ever right. The day we ate your favourite food for supper was the day it stopped being your favourite food.'

'Can we not discuss my religion?' I say.

He sighs. 'I was talking about veal.'

'You're criticizing.'

'I'm talking. You're unhappy. Now it's medical school. It's not right for you, you say. You say you want to drop out. I'm not criticizing, I'm just trying to process all this information.'

'What information?' I say. I drop-kick a pinecone into the reservoir.

'That is everybody's drinking water, young lady,' he says.

I apologize.

'As a baby, you were all right,' he says. 'You laughed when we played with you and ate all your food and went right to sleep. You used to talk and tell us everything you knew. Then you taught yourself Japanese. You did. Lovely language. Your mother and I just find you're getting increasingly complicated. Like this not wanting to be a doctor, which you have wanted since you were four.'

This is true. 'I have this tiredness,' I say.

When we get home, my dad tells my mom all the things about me he's just been telling me, and she laughs. 'I still remember all the words!' she says. '*Sumimasen. Arigato gozaimasu.*'

'*Momo,*' says my sister. 'I can still count to twenty. You made us all learn, zealot.'

'You could never keep anything to yourself,' my mom says. 'You were always improving people. You could never just leave them alone.'

'You tried to love everyone,' my sister says. 'The paperboy and the prime minister and that boy who dumped you in eleventh grade and that girl in the special class with one eye. Are you really dropping out?'

'Lies, all lies,' I say.

* * *

John has the main floor, the guts of a house twenty minutes or so east of me. I don't know who lives above or below, who could bear it. The place is old bourgeoisie, with gingerbreading and milky pink-plum stained glass, but a choking smell of peanuts and cat meat and garbage prevails, as though released by the thaw. Through the front window, a chiaroscuro vision – stained walls, books split and fallen, a mattress in front of the TV. John is standing in the inner darkness, feeding from a white box on the ironing board and watching CNN. I can't hear what he's saying.

I touch the doorframe with my knuckles, then knock twice. Deuteronomy: *The Lord shall smite thee with madness, and blindness, and astonishment of heart.* 'Gwen!' he says.

I have been spading back days, tunnelling through the weeks and months. I have been living like in a cave. 'East meets west,' I say, and he laughs, as though my nonsense is better than most. 'You're a mess, aren't you.'

'What are you going to do about it?' he asks, delighted.

He's so weak. By the time I'm finished, he won't know himself.

AWAKE

Saturday morning, six a.m. Katy is nesting seriously on the couch in the den, with the TV on soft. She has sheets, blankets. The TV has tennis. The windows are squares and shapes of sun. Katy is awake.

Her father looks in. He's a graphic designer, born in Australia, otherwise bear-like in every aspect – the beard, the hug, all of that.

'Forty love,' Katy says. 'South Africa serving for the set.' She hauls her legs in – folds – so he can sit down, which he does, prodding behind him first for her feet, watching the TV. She's little for her thirteen years, skinny and behind in terms of other girls she knows. They listen to the pop of the ball, the pretty pairs of numbers as spoken by an Englishman.

Katy's dad wakes up and looks at the watch on his wrist. Seven fifteen. 'Froot Loops,' he says.

Katy snuggles herself down into a smaller pile in her bedding. Her stomach is a knot, her fist clenched in a tennis grip. 'Oh, Dad, no.'

'I *should* make you eat.'

'Gag, vomit,' she says. 'Sadist.'

An hour later she's at the kitchen sink, chasing toast with chalky swallows of Maalox. Her girl has advanced to the semis. 'Semis,' she whispers. She dresses in bathing suit, T-shirt, shorts and sneakers. She talcs her feet up first, because she anticipates being barefoot, later, at the gym.

In the car, she clutches her car bear in her lap. This is a small-size teddy, maybe eight inches long, with a yellow terry head, green ears, red paws, a clown's suit and ruff. She won't sit in a car unless she can hold her bear. It's a problem. 'Brake!' she shouts, panicking.

Her dad eases the car around a corner. He tries to drive like silk. Today there is an open house at the Rec Centre and Katy wants to go. Gymnastics, suddenly. 'Brake!' she shouts. She closes her eyes.

'Trampoline,' he says, trying to make a picture in her mind. But she says, 'It's not that kind of gymnastics.'

At the Centre, first, is the rhythmic gymnastic display. Then other girls can try. Katy's dad watches from the bleachers, Katy from the floor, impatient. The gymnastics girls have their hair in buns and doilies; they have jewels for eyes. They bend like gum. They're even younger and smaller and prettier than Katy. Their ankles are expertly taped.

After the display they keep on stretching and hog the apparatus. Katy wants to try a ribbon. Finally she goes up to the smallest girl and asks.

'It's my own,' the girl says. She stirs the wand, sends the red ribbon licking. Then she offers it to Katy. It's heavy. Katy squiggles a couple of S's down the floor and hands it off. A little Chinese girl tosses it in the air, holds her hand out – down it comes trailing like a big sperm, like the future falling back at them: yes, she thinks this way, the melodrama of thirteen – and catches it behind her back. 'Olivia, fuck!' someone says.

Katy finds her dad. He clambers down the bleachers and picks her off the ground in a hug. 'That was so great, you sharing!'

'Dad, for Christ's sake,' she says, flushing.

* * *

Outside, later, the day has gotten scruffy. Katy's dad squires her down to the outdoor pool. She likes her sports, does Katy. Exhaustion stills her mind. 'Whoa,' she says, batting teddy's head on her knee.

The pool has a concrete bunker for changing, but Katy strips in the car. Shivering, she darts to the pool, finds her place, and joins the other girls ploughing the lanes of water.

Katy's dad watches for a minute from behind the green chain-link fence. He hacks out his own distances weekday lunch hours at the Aquatic Centre, downtown, while Katy's sucking orange squirt from a drink box with the other Rapunzels in the brand new junior high school.

He goes back to the car for his thermos. Katy's clothes are on the front passenger seat, her seat, with her watch and her bear. She has a corduroy purse with a big flap, for her keys and antacid tablets and an old postcard from Monterey.

He takes his coffee back to the fence. The swimmers are practising flip turns, like baby seals. They erupt into butterfly.

A couple of mothers are there, in down vests and Ray-Bans, like cool alien mothers. 'Hey, you guys!' one says to Katy's dad. 'How've you two been? We keep meaning to have the pair of you for supper.'

He looks at the pool, where his daughter is savaging her way through her environment with a kickboard. He nods. 'Well, Katy's going through an eating thing right now.'

The women look at him.

'Not that kind of eating thing,' he says.

* * *

Back in the car, Katy swaddles herself in towels and demands the heater. Rain droplets bloom silently on the windshield.

'Debbie Connoly gets two parties this summer,' she says. 'One for each long weekend, no parents, girl-boy, yada yada.'

'You can have a party,' Katy's dad says.

'Look, see, an invitation,' she says. 'A computer-generated invitation.' She crumples the printed card and blasts it into the nether regions, the back seat. 'Rocket ship,' she says.

'Boys, is it?'

'Oh, Debbie Connoly,' Katy says. 'Debbie Connoly should moisturize.'

At an intersection, a squeegee boy approaches. His pants ride low on his hips. When he gestures, Katy's dad shakes his head. The boy shrugs, lips moving. He's singing. Katy rolls down the window so they can hear. He's growling a slow tune, shaking his head in mockery of the drivers, rolling his eyes and grinning at the clouds.

Katy is scornful. 'Get some Benylin, there, guy.'

'He's doing Louis Armstrong.'

'I know what he's doing,' Katy says. 'Run him down.'

Katy's dad slips them into gear. She convulses, bracing elbows and knees. She blows out imaginary candles.

'Cool your jets, Dilley,' he says.

* * *

III

After soup, she takes her headphones and a certain cassette back to the couch and listens to her favourite song three times. She has a skill, verging on the mystical, which is that she can rewind her little player without reference to counter or second hand and always land at the beginning of her song.

The song itself is a searing, noisy vector, something about time and a girl. The singer is obviously in a great deal of pain and sexual frustration. It's her favourite. She doesn't think of herself as someone in a great deal of pain and sexual frustration, although she's jumpy as a bug and sometimes at night she's afraid to be alone. Is this the beginning?

'Bam,' she says, making a little explosion with her fingers. She listens to the song again.

* * *

Eleven p.m. Way up the ladder of channels, she finds an old movie – *Robin Hood*. Hats, in this movie, are very green.

Her dad joins her. He's eating from a bowl of crunchy granola. Men are dropping from the trees. He has a secret in his pocket.

'Errol Flynn,' Katy says. 'Died in the arms of a rent boy at the Sylvia Hotel.'

'Thank you,' he says.

Katy thinks about the thing he calls her, being Australian – *Kite*. Remembers the day, the moment, she realized this was not a nickname, but just the way his strange mouth made the word that was her name. She was five.

He's trying to show her something. She switches channels, pops onto the kinetic elegance of a basketball game. 'I'm pumped!' she says. She likes the tight, fast, high-walled world of the basketball court, as opposed to the vast, aimless greens of soccer where the wind blows through and the players could walk away, right out of the arena, just like that.

'Do you still want a purple bedroom?'

Paint chips, he's trying to show her.

They settle on the cartoon channel. The cartoon is a tragedy. A kitten is washed into the river. The other cats gather on the bridge. The cats stand on their hind legs and wear waistcoats. There is a high, pale fruit of a moon. The city of cats is like a cat Venice, with punts and cathedrals and inlaid cartoon piazzas. It's a night city, with shadows and torchlight, silvers and greys. The cats speak Japanese.

Katy's dad is leaning forward, his mouth open. 'This is a bloody work of art,' he says.

'I'll tell you what, though,' Katy says, fingering the paint chips. 'I'd like a dress this colour for Debbie Connoly's party.'

He looks from her to the cats, back and forth. 'Really?'

'Really, no.' She lies back and closes her eyes, flipping channels by sound until she recovers the basketball.

By one in the morning they're playing the guessing game. Katy's dad is lying on his back on the rug. Katy is still riding her couch like a barque, eyes wide open. 'Are you alive?' she asks.

'No.'

'Rock star?'

He grins, eyes closed. 'Yeh.'

'Oh, bum, the sixties,' Katy says. She reaches under her T-shirt to massage the place, just below her sternum, where it feels as though she has a hot painful plum. A tiny baby ulcer, the specialist said. Maalox was the ticket.

She closes her eyes, gives up.

★ ★ ★

Katy's dad looks at the watch on his wrist – twenty to three. They live like this, in humps and jumps, in the ads, the hours like stepping stones to the possibility of sleep. Katy's found hers, finally, on the couch again. Her bedroom frightens her lately; he doesn't know why. If he leaves the room or puts out the lights or turns off the TV she'll wake up, and it will start all over again. It tires him out, day after day, waiting for her to realize she can relax and nothing will change.

He closes his eyes, tries to get where she is.

PLAY

I

The week Martin is off in Italy, she begins to eat like a student again. She sits on the floor in the honeycomb of glass cubes which is their house, chewing Mr Noodles and little red Spartans. The honeycomb clots onto a cliff over the ocean. To visit them, you take an elevator which sets you in their living room.

They are both lawyers, hence this business of the apples is unnecessary. But the way he slops food around, wine in the vegetables. His copper pans, hung and preening. He has taken an airplane to the opera.

'I have candles somewhere,' she had said. Martin sat in her apartment. They had just met. Martin didn't like sitting on the floor, couldn't settle his knees, but she had no chairs apart from the piano bench, which was tucked under the piano. She had an air mattress and a sleeping bag. She was camping.

He could not comprehend such a sad manner of living. But he also had an old small feeling of safety, something of heat and soap, sleep and lunch. Perhaps it was the novelty of clean light on a first night.

They live together, now: he and she and the piano. She had the grand when she had nothing – black and cocked, three brass feet. She lugs it everywhere, although her ambitions are ash and she now mocks her years of practice, under the tutelage of a hobgoblin named Flannery.

Her name is Hero. She knows the stories: Hero and Claudio, Hero and Leander. But she thinks her name is not more strange than Sita, say, or Miriam.

Sita was Martin's first love. She and Martin have remained friends. She and Hero have become friends also. When she phones she says, 'Hero! Here is Sita.'

Miriam, Martin's ex-wife, would not go to Verona to sit on rocks and watch opera. Nor will Hero. 'What is stopping you from going alone?' she asked him.

Something had been stopping him. Something should be stopping him, but he cannot think what. He has money and his firm owes him time. There are no kiddies to juggle, nobody is dying, there is no one out there in his life's net who cannot spare him for a week.

* * *

Rome is a surprise. Martin expected rusticity, quantities of rough black wool, a certain sloppiness of breasts. Instead he spies trim young Romans, dark heads and pudding skin. They are uniformly slender, beautifully garbed, coiffed and shod.

Still, the city frets him until he cannot concentrate. Pigeons, beggars, priests – yes, yes. But Italian money is silly and all the famous sites look like pictures of themselves. Heat plaques him with sweat. He sees actual gypsies, a woman in the shadow of a column trying to breastfeed a child of three or four. The child's blond head lolls, it has one pit and one eye. The city writhes with cats.

He thinks he could like it here in winter.

* * *

Sita comes to visit. She steps from the elevator in clothes the colour of sand, bringing pears and a pack of brown sugar. 'I'm going to make you a crumble,' she says.

Hero eats a white slice of pear, luscious and gritty. She watches Sita whisk brown goo in one of Martin's pans on a ring of his nubby blue flames. 'Now, what's all this,' Sita says.

Hero can't tell if she's talking to her or the goo. 'He'll be back,' she says, guessing. 'It's just for a week.'

'There's nothing in your fridge.'

Sita's husband is Salm. Sita and Salm own a restaurant called Pan-Pan. You can eat chocolate things there, also bamboo and curries. It's a narrow, fashionable restaurant with one table in the window. Rich schoolgirls go there for Darjeeling at dusk.

The crumble is warm and lovely, fragrant with cloves but not too sweet. The women eat. Sita, washing up, will not hear of help, so Hero watches the afternoon movie on the big blue television. The movie is in black and white, with serious men in hats and trench coats shooting at men in black cars, and women with hats and furs looking weepy and pouring drinks and explaining at great length about someone named Floyd who never showed up. They all sipped their drinks and said that Floyd was certainly a rat.

'Come look at this,' Hero calls to Sita.

Sita comes and perches on the arm of the sofa, watching.

'They have little ladies' guns in those handbags,' Hero says. 'For delicate shooting.'

'I might have a baby,' Sita says.

Why does this make Hero so happy, so carbonated with pleasure? Of course the baby is Salm's. It will have damp black hair and a baby's goofy giggle. Sita will be an excellent mother. 'You will be an excellent mother,' Hero says. 'What's this "might"?'

'Can I use your phone?'

Martin and Hero almost met at Pan-Pan. They sat back to back, alone, alone. Hero listened to Martin and the waitress, who seemed to know one another. She brought their black coffees and bills at the same time. They bumped chairs getting up and smiled like good people, but Hero busted their groove by going to the washroom.

'Can I use your phone?'

Last night he phoned from Italy. She said, 'Here we are, speaking across vast distances.'

'*No, no,*' he said. She understood he was not talking to her. '*Si, no.* Go away.'

'Are you on the street?'

'I just ate melon,' he said. 'I have to go line up soon.'

'Good!' she said encouragingly.

Hero and Martin met on the pavement outside Pan-Pan. Martin waited, slowly decking himself with scarf, gloves. It was not the first time he had seen her there. He would have spoken to her, suggested they sit together, but for Sita, his happy mother owl.

'I have candles somewhere,' she said a little later.

And now she lives in his house, this Hero, this peanut butter brunette who once, when he had flu, made him a citrus salad with squashy hunks of grapefruit, orange and lemon.

'Can I use your phone?' Sita says.

* * *

The German bus pulls into Verona at dawn. Martin has somehow bought the last seat on a tour from Stuttgart, which left his Roman hotel late last night. He feels he has arrived by the skin of his teeth. The air is moty and golden, the land dry but tended and yielding; he suspects the proximity of grapes. Breakfast is blood orange juice and coffee.

When Hero moved in, he thought she would need a day to unpack, to settle in, in fact to browse. He closed himself into his study, forced himself to leave her alone. She put her Noxzema by the sink and hung her loofah on a prong. She set her iron tablets in the kitchen cupboard and laid her black tights, polar socks and white 'Madrid '04' T-shirt on the bed. These were her pyjamas. Other things she pushed under the bed, out of sight. She went to find him. 'Hi,' she said. The next morning she did the dishes, dried the sink, made the bed and put her pyjamas back in her suitcase, back under the bed. 'You just got here!' Martin said. She didn't understand.

His house is a lonely glass Rubik's cube with too many perspectives on the ocean. Two rooms have no windows: the kitchen, birch, granite and brushed steel, humming like the bridge of a spaceship; and the bedroom, one wall studded with blue aquariums, like portholes below a waterline. You have to go behind the wall to get at the tanks. This is a long narrow space, fluorescent and bubbling, reminiscent of the TV wall in a department store. Both Martin and Hero like to feed the fish. Consequently there are many deaths from glut – an excuse to buy more. They buy black, gold and red tetras. These are wee and cheap and their deaths seem no more than blown matches.

Miriam was an engineer. She had a hard hat. She died of a heart attack, most unusual, but not until long after the divorce, when she was living in Brazil. Martin rarely thinks of her now, except when he travels.

During the bad time with Miriam, Martin fled to New York to

hear Georgia Andersson at the Met in *Lucia di Lammermoor*. It snowed. He collected pens and postcards, papery stamps and a cup of drink. He sat in his hotel room, writing at the writing table by the window. 'I like it here,' he wrote, crying. Outside, it snowed on New York. Below him, cars knifed slices down the white roads. That night he slept like a child.

In the early morning, Martin walks around the two-thousand-year-old arena, where the opera will be staged that evening. The Veronese are on their way to work. A tall, slim, ugly woman in crocodile heels, sage linen suit and gold necklet stands before the arena, arguing in tongues into a black wafer of a cell phone.

Martin and Hero do not argue, exactly. But the piano stays locked and her possessions are absurdly few. She will not spread herself, she is always tidying, she stores books and socks and tea in her knapsack under the bed. Martin is the tourist, the lover of music, but Hero is the traveller. The piano stays locked, the bags stay packed. She will not play.

* * *

Plus she is a rotten lawyer. Telephones make her nervous.

'Sure,' she says to Sita a few days later, clutching the receiver too tightly. 'Whenever is fine.' Hanging up, she goes into the tank room behind the bedroom, skims half a dozen dead tetras and flushes them down the toilet, a toilet she cannot bring herself to use.

There was a time when she carried Bach on the bus and patched her jeans with silver duct tape. Flannery would tell her what she was doing wrong. Sucking your cheeks in like *this*, Flannery would say. Tensing your elbows like *this*. Flannery said Hero at her instrument had the poise of a chimp.

One autumn day, an improbable varsity autumn of blue skies, wood smoke and Rossetti auburns, Hero drifted, numb from a lesson, past a line-up of what, upon closer inspection, proved to be the preppiest, most nervous people she had ever encountered. They were LSAT candidates and their hour was nigh.

PRE-REGISTERED, said a sign over a Dantesque snake of lives in balance.

WALK-IN, said another, so she did.

She ended up at a desk next to a boy in a red blazer and jeans. He loaned her an extra sharp pencil. 'Well, there's a logic section,' he said, pale and swallowing. 'There's a language comprehension section.'

Halfway through the exam he dropped his booklet and fled. Hero spent the next three hours happily doodling little lines of six cows. 'If the cow furthest to the left has spots and not less than three cows are female, and no Jersey may stand next to a heifer....' She passed with cymbals and streamers and allowed her hands' muscles to atrophy into mouse flesh.

For a while, then, she was a woman in a gold trench coat with a herringbone umbrella who bought white tubes of coloured shampoo and lived on *sabji* and oranges. Pan-Pan satisfied her taste for basil *naan*, so she became something of a regular.

Secretly, Martin hates and fears her LSAT story. It is the thread, spit-delicate, from which his life hangs.

* * *

Sita takes a rare pleasure in the telephone. Cross-legged on the carpet in tights the colour of meal and a long fine sweater of iron-hued silk, she calls her wholesaler. 'Yes, it's not a problem,' she says. 'Next week is highly unlikely.'

Friday, and Sita is back. Hero sits in the cedar chair, reading her herb book and being near, for Sita and Salm have had a blow. Sita's white suede backpack is already stashed in the guest bedroom.

Sita dials a number, immediately cuts it off with her finger and hesitates. She does not look at Hero. Hero is conscious of not being looked at. *It is traditional*, says Hero's book, *for the woman of the house to keep her herb garden near the kitchen door, handy for cuttings, remedies and refuge.* Hero has such a garden, despite her orbital kitchen. It is as near to the kitchen door as she can make it; that is, a patch of good earth at the top of the elevator, near the gravel spread where they station the cars. Up here it's flat and sunny but sheltered from the wind by sappy pines, with a conquistador's view of the ocean.

Hero cultivates the usual greenery – curling, aromatic and

shrubby. Three bristling bushes of Tuscan rosemary in terracotta pots, Martin's gift at sixty dollars a pop, thrive perversely and smell celestial.

'Martin says *buon giorno*.'

Sita has surfaced from the elevator, cigarette already in her teeth. She leans forward, frowning, flicks a flame from her fist and sucks it up into her cigarette. Gaspers, Salm calls them. Hero crushes a blade of mint and sniffs her fingers and thumb. Sita is now wearing a white cricketing sweater with a thick garnet V over her previous clothes.

'I picked up the phone and there he was. It didn't even ring.'

'Instant Martin.' Hero fingers some dry earth, knowing dry is good. The rosemary likes dry.

Sita shivers. 'There's a wind up.'

'Storm.' Hero points to black sky blooming.

'Speaking of which,' Sita says, 'I should phone that Salm.'

Back in the house, she peels out of Martin's sweater and drops it on the sofa. 'Are you hungry?' she asks Hero. 'I can do this thing with an egg.'

'Phone your man,' Hero says.

Hero and Martin do not argue, exactly. But he throws himself everywhere, his lines are tangled up in everything. He takes a magpie's hoarding delight in olives, in sunlight and fine old voices. He casts his affections loose and wide, and claims the better part of the world.

* * *

After the opera, back in his hotel room, Martin has a garbled impression of gongs and trumpets, soda vendors and headdresses, thin pure voices threading up out of the arena. He bought a program and a sandwich, and a couple of birthday candles with a slip of paper, like from a fortune cookie but printed with *Arena di Verona* instead of a fortune, in a stapled plastic bag. Around him they lit the candles, to pretty effect as night came down. He will take his candles home, a souvenir for Hero. 'I have candles somewhere,' she had said.

The opera singers parade through Martin's dreams in long

coloured cloaks, blue alto, green bass. They are twelve feet tall and have escaped from the arena. He follows them down cobbled streets, wants to guide them back, but they walk faster and faster, trailing their fingertips along the warm stone walls in a way that is oddly familiar.

* * *

The storm hits silently – snow.

Hero tries to watch the snow accumulate, but the snow will not be serious. It falls slowly in large papery flakes that vanish in the sea.

Sita stands, knapsack slung from one silk shoulder, pressing for the elevator. 'I'm to come home directly and immediately, before the roads slick up. He's delighted about the baby really, it was just a shock.' She smooths her hair, preening unconsciously, like a bird.

Go on, Sita, Hero is thinking. Get along, you elevator Madonna.

The elevator cage arrives and Sita steps inside, closing the wrought iron gate. She points at Hero's grand before disappearing through the ceiling. 'Did you really play that thing?' she calls.

'Well, I tried,' Hero says.

There is a second way out of the glass house: a long flight of wooden steps, pine-hemmed, ricketing down to a pocket of stony beach. This is a place forever cold and dripping, quietly rank, scribbled with kelp. Sometimes Hero comes down with a cheese bun and Martin's opera glasses to look for whales.

BEACH ACCESS boasted the realtor's blurb. Martin has never set foot on it. Looking for Hero, he would jog three-quarters of the way down the stairs, stoop, squint, sniff, and rattle the railing as though he were trying to shake its hand, whereupon he would turn around and jog back up into the belly of his warm glass cubes, his house.

Martin's money is such that he works when he wants to.

The waves lick coldly, as though Hero is watching a film of the waves and the sound is piped in from another place. She stands hugging herself there until she imagines she can hear the phone ringing, far above.

* * *

The next night, after the opera, Martin arrives at a certain *trattoria*, a place he knows he will never find again in this life; the streets would slink into new configurations just to hide it from him. The walls are lined with bottles. His waiter takes a pale wine from the ceiling with six-foot pincers. Martin tastes colours. Somehow he procures crusty bread and olives, slabs of roast eggplant and *pâté*. Outside, the hot rain. Inside, for a *dolce*, he is given a pear. He pours more wine. The pear sits on a plate with a small sharp knife.

At the next table, a man studies a photograph. He arrived when Martin did, kept pace with him through supper, staring at this photograph the whole time. Now he takes a mouthful of red wine, swallows, and coughs like a dog. He looks up at Martin. 'Come from the opera?' he says in English.

Martin nods.

'That could break your heart.'

'It could,' Martin agrees.

'My wife,' he says, waving the photo – some order of blonde. The man himself is large, sleepy-eyed, with the creased good looks of an Irish film star.

'Martin,' says Martin.

'Caper Drake,' says the man.

'Caper Drake?' says Hero an hour later. 'What is he, a duck detective?'

'How's my harem?'

'Sita split.'

'Story of my life, alas,' says Martin. 'And what about Hero?'

'I'm just waiting,' Hero says.

* * *

She is gone, she is gone – that is the gist of it. 'Broach the red,' the man recommends. They order a carafe, and another, while his Irish tongue unspools the ruination of their love. Martin is a sucker for all opera, the rhetoric and equipment of it; even sober, he believes in the aristocracy of men in love, and it is long past midnight, and he is far from sober. Love, death, and love again – no, Martin absolutely cannot allow him to pay the bill.

As he withdraws his wallet, silence falls around them like

cloth. The man watches him, toying with the pear knife. Martin realizes they are alone in the restaurant, have been alone for a long time, and the big Italian waiters are leaning against the door.

'I don't have a wife, you idiot,' the man says.

Martin's mind scribbles back to Hero. 'What do you want?' he asks, trying to see the bones of the situation, its basic terms, although he realizes, now, he has been floating for days. The waiters watch them from the doorway, arms barred with towels. 'Money?'

He shrugs. 'I won't say no.'

Martin thumbs off a number of bills.

'Do you have a picture of your woman?' the man asks. 'I'll take that, too.'

'My what?' Martin says, starting to laugh.

* * *

Hero in her little car throws along over the bridge. Her chest is fluttering, the sky is torn gold foil. Her fingers sweep the stereo like Braille. Around her, brake lights splash and dim, although oncoming headlights are weak as breath. The hour is turning. She feels she is driving through water.

In front of the fish store, she tucks her car neatly into a hole in a line of cars. She became ever so much better at parallel parking after Martin taught her to use her bumpers. 'Give him a little kiss,' he would say, meaning the car behind.

An hour ago, on the phone, Martin had told her some odd story about an excellent wine and a man who took his *lira*.

'He also wanted a picture of you,' Martin said.

'Me?'

'It's his system, I guess. I gave him a picture of Sita.'

'You carry a picture of Sita?'

'Not any more.'

'That's tidy,' Hero said, raising her voice. 'Has she been phoning you? You know she's been practically living here?'

'Of course,' Martin said. 'I asked her to check on you and feed you if necessary. You're screaming at me, are we arguing?'

'I'm going out right now to buy some more fish. I'm buying

angels this time and I want you to leave them alone.'

'Hey,' Martin said.

'Damn right, hey. These are going to be my fish, and if you send Sita or anyone to feed them, I'm gone.'

Martin thought of Sita, imagined the man showing her picture after supper, calling her his wife; imagined Hero striding through the fish store, trailing her fingertips along the tanks until she reached the angels, where the clerk wielded a skimmer and a plump baggy of clean aquarium water. 'That one's mine,' Hero would say, stabbing a finger at the glass, at the black suck-faced creatures trailing veils and fins. 'That one and that one.'

He wondered how much longer they would be together. He wondered and she heard it, clean across the world.

II

Martin and Hero don't have children, but Martin has an imaginary daughter named Claudia. She has clipped hair and a pure skin, and will study political science or architecture. She will drink beers and make love, sometimes in a blue dress.

Dad, she will say. Oh, dad.

* * *

She collects him from the airport, by the carousels. He's wearing new brown shoes.

'What else is Italy for?' he asks.

'What did you bring me?'

He wants to embrace her, his only child. What indeed?

She vanishes as Hero, throng-dodging, seizes him in a vicious, luscious hug.

'Hey,' he says into her hair.

'Hey, new shoes!' she says. 'How was the opera?'

Claudia, supplanted, loiters by a pillar. Tall, when did she get so tall?

'Loud. No survivors.'

'That's what I like to hear,' says Hero.

Driving, she gives news. That is, she holds up two fingers. Martin touches her index finger.

'Sita's pregnant.'

'I know.' Too late, he bites, savages, his tongue. Oh well.

* * *

While he is kissing her back, she flexes her wrists, ankles, feels many neat little pops and snaps.

'Quit wiggling,' he says.

The bedroom is cool and dark, but it's too early for all this, still light beyond the walls. Now I'll never get to sleep, thinks Hero, and I'll be sand-eyed tomorrow. Your jet lag, love, is screwing us both.

She arches her spine, blades her shoulders, tests her joints for click.

'Heard that,' he says.

She gets on her back and they finish quickly.

'I should start running again,' she says. 'My skeleton is audible and I want a tan. Also I'm going to reorder the bookshelves and paint the living room. Pretty soon I'll have an affair, twins, and give up law to become an astronaut. Are you listening to me? I'm thinking to have the piano tuned.'

'Yes!' Martin says, already asleep.

* * *

Late morning finds Claudia crabby, Martin genial, Hero gone – her office is downtown and she likes to beat the morning bridge jam. He shaves, showers, and shoves himself dry with her towel, although his own, clean and green, is ready on the bar.

By ten-thirty the house brims with light in unfamiliar places. He cuts a sandwich and takes it to eat in the living room, just to admire the planks of morning sun laid out on the carpet. Here Claudia, zebra-striped, sits on the floor in an old cable-knit sweater of his, bleached jeans, and two pairs of socks. She cuddles a mug of tea in her palms and plays at dipping her toes in and out of the sun.

'Well, we're back, hooray,' she says.

'For sure, hooray!' he says. 'What is this? Sarcasm?'

'Miss me?' And she's gone.

The sealed black grand stands tiptoe in the corner, brass key slot glittering, feet in shade. It reminds him of something he read once, that a car doing ninety has, at any given time, an entire area of contact with the road no larger than the palm of a hand.

* * *

Whenever it was she first appeared – he can't remember – Claudia was always his daughter, never his wife. Wives had tanned knees and snacked on broccoli florets. Their underwear was *chartreuse*, maybe, or *sky*. Claudia wore yellow pyjamas with feet and cuddled in his lap with a blue blanket. When he put her to bed he wrapped her in the blanket and thus she slept, in sweet fragility, almost breathing.

* * *

Maybe she came during Hero's move from her tony Kits condo just a toss from the sea to Martin's more austere glass palace. Hero had insisted on renting a U-Haul for all but the piano, eating Vietnamese take-out after the kitchen was packed, boxing and stuffing and taping with relish, leaving without a backward glance. She surrendered the keys while he was struggling with some bungee cords, so that he never saw the inside of the place again. He had wanted a last look round, but she wanted to be gone. This difference between them depressed him.

They drove the U-Haul to Spanish Banks and sat on the hood, leaning against the windshield, eating greasy fish and chips from a cardboard box and drinking lime sodas. The setting sun made shadow bowls in the sand.

Martin, miserable, squished a blurb of ketchup from a plastic envelope onto his chips. Hero sucked a Fudgesicle with obnoxious glee.

'I'm glad you're coming,' he said.

'I like moving.'

'We had good times there.'

'Sure, but I like *moving*.'

He watched a family by the shore, calling to each other with the clear, meaningless voices of birds. Mother and son wading, daughter and black dog chasing seagulls. 'Here! Here!' the father said. The birds cried and cried.

Maybe that was the day she came, the little one at the beach.

* * *

When he was small, Martin was taken to the symphony, the opera, the Early Music Society, the Recital Society, and the Choral Society. Once, at a premiere of new works by local composers, his father took him backstage to have his program autographed by the pianist, a stern young Irishwoman with a pronounced limp.

'What a bat,' young Martin said, although he kept Flannery's autograph for many years.

* * *

Claudia's childhood, in fact, was not much different from Martin's, except he was the father and she loved every minute of it.

* * *

So what was this boyhood he craved? Summers pumping gas on the Trans-Canada, perhaps – browning your biceps selling worms to anglers and cream sodas to sun-woozed sweets in cutoffs – piny forests, pit toilets, forest fire warnings, bear warnings, horsefly warnings, no-lifeguard warnings, poisonous berry warnings, bold bracing summer lungfuls of the great Canadian outdoors....

* * *

(This, in fact, was Hero's adolescence in Hope, B.C. – a biggish, squarish town stuffed up the crotch of the Fraser Canyon – for the two summers her parents rented a house there. Flat, far-from-the-sea, fast-food Hope – she pumped gas, browned her biceps, practised the piano, drank beer with some local fat girls, and was bored out of her mind. Hero hated Hope, hated her parents, her friends, her clothes, her hair, her house, her music, hated everything with a meticulousness that boded well for her as-yet-inconceivable future in law.)

Back from her run, she finds him out on the deck, organizing Thai. The barbecue yawns, a black mouthful of coals. On its wing tray, a sleeve of bamboo skewers awaits satay. Chunks of chicken, festive peppers and coconut meats bedeck many saucers. Tied sheaves of lemon grass stand by.

Grabbing a fork, she spikes a blister on her heel, presses out water.

'Someone called about a shower for Sita,' Martin says, crunching a green triangle of raw pepper. 'Also a message from Sikora's, those CDs you ordered are in. Sweet thing, that is officially your fork.'

The sun is white through closed lids. The surf booms far below. A deep, dangerous, satisfying *poof* signals Martin has torched the barbecue.

'You gonna shower?'

Talc and deodorant, teak-handled hairbrush, drawer full of clean white cotton sensibles. In her closet are polo shirts in melon shades, crinkly chinos, comfy bronze summer flats. On her dresser, in a porcelain rice-bowl, the gold watch, gold bracelet, gold band.

'Nah, think I'll eat sweaty,' she says.

* * *

A few minutes pass. Martin tips his head to watch a jet spew skyward. He's thinking dragonflies, cruciforms, stars in the East, when memory hits. 'I invited Sita and Salm.'

'Well,' she says, hauling up.

* * *

In a rugby shirt striped navy and custard she stand, hands on hips, legs and feet bare, surveying the closet.

'My, what shanks,' Martin says.

'I'm strong, but Sita's always so smooth. You think maybe a sarong under this?'

'You want?'

Tomorrow is Monday again – wasn't it Monday just yesterday?

OXYGEN

She imagines a two-day week, a lifetime of Sundays and Mondays, and despairs.

'Get out,' she says. 'I can't do this with you looking at me.'

He sits down on the bed.

* * *

Dinner: Sita, Salm, Martin, Hero and Claudia.

'You're not showing yet, though,' Hero is saying.

'I am, I am!' Sita says. The women leave for the bedroom, for Sita to show off her showing.

Martin and Salm lean back expansively – they're both a little buzzed. Martin is shorter, leaner; Salm is tall, a devilish looker, too good to be true. Black eyes, lashes, curls, muscled like a discus thrower under his white cotton shirt, madras shorts, and surf sandals.

'Salm, you progenitor, you,' Martin says.

Salm smiles. 'I'm scared shitless, I assure you.' His accent is pure Oxford. 'What if it turns out to be, I don't know, a serial killer or an accountant or something?'

'Worse things than serial killers.'

'Oh, you guys.' Claudia, tomboy twelve, sits on the deck rail, swinging a bare foot. She's a little in love with Salm, the movie star aspect, although she mocks his accent ruthlessly. 'I'm *ever so* hungry.'

'Almost ready,' her father says.

* * *

'I have *never* seen *anyone* do *that* before,' Sita says to Martin at the barbecue.

Hero has just lit the citronellas. Martin whisks and drizzles, showing off. Sita pokes him in the arm until he feeds her something off a fork.

Salm leans close. 'Do you suppose they're having an affair?'

'Absolutely,' Hero says, disliking him.

'Think we should break it up?'

Hero sticks two fingers in her mouth and gives a raunchy whistle. Sita and Martin look over, smiling. Hero wags a warning finger

130

at Martin, who gives her a little wave.

Salm is delighted with the whistle. 'Girls can do that?'

'Well, see, I'm half boy. On my father's side.'

'Teach me!' he begs. 'I'll use your fingers!'

Hero shrugs and sips her pineapple juice. She needs to cry, suddenly, but – here, in her house, with her husband and friends – she has nowhere to go.

* * *

The summer Hero turned thirteen, she passed from childhood into the tight pale funk of adolescence. She had lost her first competition in June.

It was hosted by a Catholic boys' school, at end of term. The audience was padded with students shepherded by their teacher, a young Québécoise in a blue cardigan whom they treated with clumsy gallantry, rude raw love. Mary, thought cool Hero, who at twelve reckoned she knew a thing or two about faith.

She played in the Open Bach class: a pensive prelude and a long unspooling fugue. With each voice she tried to imitate the tone of another instrument – oboe, flute, the husky slicing of a cello. She bound them together as she had been taught, highlighting colours here and there, knotting the lines at cadences, until she reached the last chord, the sound's hem. As she stood, in the precise moment before applause, she heard the click of Flannery's cassette recorder.

The other competitor, the winner, played a toccata which proceeded like flame down a fuse.

The adjudicator, a bearded trombonist from the Vancouver Symphony Orchestra, gave them each a page of notes and a sticker. 'I made MUSIC today!' said Hero's sticker. The other girl's said 'First'.

One after another, the boys filed up to them. 'I thought you played really well,' they said to Hero. 'That was good,' they said to Jordan, the other girl.

'You played better than me,' Hero said.

'I love your shoes,' Jordan said. 'I want your hair.'

* * *

'Quit picking on her, Salm.'

'No, that's all right, pick on her,' Martin says.

After their meal of crisp meats, bright vegetables and soft breads, they carried the citronella buckets into the living room as a chill wind reared with the darkness. Now they're standing in puddles of moon, staring at Hero. Salm and Martin want her to play.

The piano is poised like something sentient – a big quiet animal, a watchful pet. Salm runs a fingertip down the length of its curve, around the back, up the straight side and back to the front, ending at the keyhole. Insolently he flips up the lid and fingers out a tiny piece of Bach, the right hand of a child's minuet, a green and yellow sound in the key of G.

'No,' Hero says.

He pulls the bench out and seats himself. 'They made me learn,' he says. 'For five years, my teacher used to eat lunch during my lessons. When she yelled at me, she'd spit little bits of sandwich onto the keyboard. I hit all these wrong notes trying to avoid them, and then she'd yell even more.' With the first three fingers of his left hand he begins, on lowest A, a quiet walk up the keyboard, sounding every key. Like a dog pissing on every hydrant, Hero thinks. Please stop touching, Salm. Please *don't*. 'Hero used to teach,' Martin says.

Briefly enough. After splitting with Flannery, the second and final time, she got a job teaching private lessons out of a preschool in Point Grey. Her students had the names the rich can afford to give their children: Gretchen, Theo, Juliet. She taught them 'Pop Goes the Weasel'; they, in turn, liked to show her their little lost teeth. At Christmas they gave her swanky gifts, pralines and hand creams, chosen by their mothers.

'Teach me something now,' Salm says.

Sita stands apart, watching.

From behind, Hero lays her arms over his arms, her hands over his hands, flattens his wrists and moulds his fingers into curves. She draws his hands from the keyboard, lays them in his lap, gently closes the lid and leaves the room.

III

There had been arguments before, of course – Flannery sleek and coiled, Hero pale with headache – but Hero had not walked out before, auditioned at the college and been accepted; and Flannery had not laughed before and said, *Whatever you want, bright angel;* so this time, for the first time, Hero was on her own.

* * *

Six hours into the day, dawn poured. Hero, straightening from a curve of sleep, swatted at her clock-radio. Bug-like, it gnawed her to consciousness.

In the kitchen her roommate, Sarah, sat with a sprout sandwich and a bottle of Kirin. Sarah worked most nights. The perfectly round frames of her glasses made her look smart, sisterly, shy. 'Are you up?' she asked softly.

Hero dragged open the fridge door, questing grimly for juice. 'All yours,' she said.

* * *

Hero and Sarah shared a bed, but this did not mean what it could have. They were poor. They had a one-bedroom apartment where Sarah slept while Hero was at school. Why should they have bought two beds when one was enough? They were both clean. They saw little enough of each other and the odd reminder – a stray sequin, a trace of blood – was small enough price to pay when you considered their prospects and ambitions. Hero was going to be a concert pianist and Sarah was a stripper.

* * *

'Try these olives,' Sarah would say, proffering a Styrofoam cup from behind her newspaper. 'This is interesting. There's this hijacking in, what, Argentina? The stewardess says, "Steak or chicken?" and the guy says, "I have bomb. We go Singapore." So she goes into the cockpit, tells the captain, comes back, and the guy goes, "Now bring me steak," and she goes, "You took too long deciding, we ran out. You're having chicken." Guess what?'

133

'What?' Hero said weakly.

'I got a raise. Really, try these olives, I think they're from Iraq? They have these tasty flecks?'

'*It's six-thirty in the morning,*' Hero said.

'He ate the chicken, too. Entire 747 at gunpoint and it didn't occur to him to swap with somebody. Want some of my carrot?'

'Go figure,' Hero said, laying her head on her arms on the table. Falling back to sleep, she dreamt briefly of keys.

* * *

By rights, Sarah ought to have looked like Hero. Hero had the curls, the eyes, the sleek smooth figure and the languid glance. Sarah's hair was fine and colourless as cat sheddings. She was skinny and nervous and her hands were always cold.

* * *

Hero'd been at it since she was three. That made eighteen years. When she practised her Hanon exercises she imagined a lead pea in each fingertip, weighting her touch. For Chopin her fingers were pencil erasers, sponge-tipped but firm. For Bartók they were drumsticks, drills, mallets, sometimes wire brushes on the imaginary snare of her keyboard. For Bach they teased out Braille trails of melody to guide her through the maze of sound.

When Hero got home she saw Sarah's hands in dishwater or painting each other's nails fudge brown. Sarah's hands were just some fingers and a thumb.

* * *

Sarah was not a stripper, although certain people construed it that way. Sarah was a belly dancer at a falafel bar owned by a Lebanese man named Gary. She worked for him every night from eleven until five. It was true that Sarah did a lot of writhing, but it was ethnic writhing and she kept her clothes on. Sometimes men would tuck dollar bills into the jingling waistband of her gauze pants, below her navel. During her coffee break she picked them out. She unfolded them and flushed any telephone numbers and presented them to Gary, who usually gave them back.

* * *

A few people wondered if Hero had what it took, including Hero. Every day she caught the bus to the college, where she had booked practice time in a studio. The studios were a row of twenty false-ceilinged cubicles in an unheated hangar mostly abandoned to storage – theatrical scenery and props, table saws, car body parts belonging to the department of sculpture. Hero had a big key for the bigger building and a smaller key that fit all the cubicles.

She wanted to work especially hard on her Beethoven. She had chosen a late sonata, the Opus 109, after attending a workshop with a eunuch from the Conservatory who said it was about death and resignation. She thought, I'll teach you to hear. But sometimes her fingers wouldn't do what she wanted them to and then she wondered.

* * *

Gary told Sarah that in the Middle East belly dancing was not a sex dance, it was art. In Saudi Arabia, a professional belly dancer could earn more than a surgeon. She could also go to prison for using her hands too suggestively or for touching herself. The dance lived and died in the hands.

Gary said Sarah was a natural and he should know, but Sarah just liked losing her mind to her body. It wasn't complicated. Sarah's work clothes were a pair of filmy aqua harem pants, gold bra and purple cloth for her head. She also wore a fake emerald on her brow and chains of silver bells around her hips and biceps and ankles. This was not traditional costume. It was Walt Disney for grown-ups, which was what the customers liked to see. When Sarah danced she was a vision, pure as a cartoon.

Back at home she wore braids and a Nike T-shirt with overalls and thick grey socks. This was her disguise.

* * *

Hero thought she could picture herself as an older woman:

She lived alone in her own house with a Bösendorfer. She would be relearning the Opus 109. Suddenly she would get a craving for Christmas oranges. She imagined making tea in a blue-and-white china pot and peeling the little oranges with her fingers. She imagined listening to Glenn Gould on the CD player and watching the snow fall. She would go to the corner store (because there would be a corner store) and buy mandarins and loose tea and bitter chocolate. When she opened the front door she would see her piano just as she left it, in the cold clear sunlight, with the Beethoven on the stand. All her life would be here.

* * *

Sarah got into belly dancing by accident. When she lived in residence at the university she signed up for a jazzercise class because she was lonely. On the first night she walked into a room containing a record player, a mirrored wall, and a woman who tossed her a big crimson veil and showed her how to fasten it in her belt and wind it up over her hair and across her face. Sarah was hooked. Over the next few months she learned to keep her shoulders still while she swished her hips. She learned to keep her face blank as a puddle and to speak with her hands. She became the dance – aloof and sinuous, open and closed.

Across the hall, they jazzed without her.

* * *

Hero's teacher at the moment was old Michael Shanagh. Mr Shanagh had seen Rubinstein in Vienna and had master classes with Richter. One day, Hero had a master class with Anton Kuerti. She was so nervous she couldn't hear or play right. Afterwards, Mr Shanagh apologized to Kuerti because he had had to listen to such a piss-poor performance. Hero didn't know how Kuerti replied but she knew she was no longer a student of Mr Shanagh's.

* * *

Her new teacher at the college was Mr Reedy, in fact Bob. When she played her Chopin étude, he staggered and bugged his eyes out and clutched at the piano like an actor in a silent film. He said he wasn't a big technique guy himself but he sure liked his students to have fun when they played. One day in lesson he asked her if she wasn't excited to be alive.

'I guess not,' Hero said. After her lesson she went to the registrar's and quit the college. She went home and vacuumed.

* * *

Sarah in daytime was like a small animal emerging through snow. She blinked at Hero, trying to remember.

* * *

Sarah saw Hero was drifting. She introduced Hero to Gary's friend Ray, who owned a record store. Ray found Hero serious and knowledgeable and a tasteful dresser. He offered her a job in Classical, top floor. In time Hero gravitated down to World, in the basement, where she could listen to reggae and bangra and flamenco all day, and no one had heard of Kuerti or Richter or the Opus 109.

Hero decided that a person's taste in music was indicative of her emotional range. She considered the piano, music you have to sit down to. She watched the other sales clerks shift and sway. She thought about Beethoven and what music was for.

She also remembered the first chord of the Opus 109. She remembered placing the left hand, a low E. The sound was like velvet, like honey, cool as water, warm as sleep. There were no words for that sound.

* * *

Hero and Sarah went to a psychic fair in a football stadium. They drank tea and tried to spot honest people. They went into a tent, pitched right there in the stadium, to have their palms read.

'Am I going to die?' Sarah asked happily. She was drunk on daylight.

The palm reader was a pale young man with intense eyes. 'What do you think?' he said. 'Of course you're going to die. Everyone dies. Hands.'

Sarah held both hands in front of her like a Christmas child. The palm reader, frowning hard, selected one and traced her palm with one finger. He told Sarah she would have passionate love with a Welsh drag queen.

'I could get into that,' Sarah said.

Slowly, Hero took her gloves off. When she offered the psychic her hand, he dismissed Sarah from the tent with the flick of one finger.

Hero's palms didn't have much skin on them. They were raw and scabbed and sticky with a clear watery pus. Lately she did this to herself and then forgot. She would also make patterns with her razors, scoring the pads of her fingers, which didn't tend to scar.

The psychic went behind a curtain and came back with a clear bottle and a white bottle and some gauze. He swabbed her palms with cotton balls soaked in rubbing alcohol, which hurt and felt good. He poured out some cream and rubbed it into each of her hands with his two hands. He bandaged her, winding the gauze round and round and fastening the ends by tucking them back into her palms, leaving her fingers free. He helped her pull her gloves back on. He looked at her face.

'Toughen up,' he said.

Outside, Sarah was scanning the crowd. 'What did he say?' she asked.

'Lots,' Hero said. 'Nothing.'

* * *

Hero and Sarah went shopping. Sarah bought nail polish and Krazy Glue and a spray for her tomato plants. Hero considered castanets, but couldn't make them go.

* * *

The next day she phoned Flannery.

IV

They sit at a café on Denman, slurping froth from their costly coffees. A mess of preschoolers in matching T-shirts lurches past. Their T-shirts are sky blue with gold suns. The suns sport sunglasses and crowns bobbled like jesters' hats.

'I quit the firm,' Hero tells Martin, who doesn't hear.

She follows his gaze to the littlest of the creatures, in snowy

138

sneakers and the elbow-swallowing shirt. She's smiling at him, just for this moment, sweet and still as a springbok.

'Sweetheart,' he says.

'I quit the firm.'

He looks up at her face. 'All right.'

'Well, ok, *quit*. Sabbatical, what have you.' She bites a nail, spits it off.

'Breakfast of champions,' he says.

* * *

Later, in bed, they listen to the rumbling tanks. 'Isn't it a little late for you to become a concert pianist?'

Webs of teal light wobble on the bed, their hands.

V

'Another thing about Salm, he's always right.'

'Men are,' Martin says.

They're sitting on Sita's made bed, hip to hip, ankles twined, Sita talking, Martin paging through a trade magazine from the restaurant, addressed to Salm. Sita barefoot, in a silk slip the colour of weak tea.

'No, I mean, he *is*,' she says. 'Anything you want to know, he already knows. Tomorrow's weather. What to do with kohlrabi. Stock exchange.'

'Handy,' Martin concedes.

'We're much better off than we should be, for restaurant people. He knows too much about everything.'

'Us?'

She shrugs.

'Hero once told me she thought being in love was like getting kicked in the head by Jesus. Good to know it exists, but you're gritting your teeth just the same.'

'She worked on that,' Sita says, without malice. Creamy with pregnancy, she can do no wrong, for him.

Martin thinks he loves everyone.

Sita takes a glass bowl of sugared yoghurt from the bedside table and spoons it up. She also likes marzipan and caramelized spaghetti. When Martin first went with her she fed him icy white wines and bowls of lemon pasta. Curry with peaches. Now her sweet tooth is vulgar and astonishing. She consumes raw forkfuls of demerara sugar, hates chocolate. She floats balls and curls of ice cream in her morning coffee.

Martin takes the bowl from her hands, disentangles his legs. 'Mmmm!' she says, frowning, a mouth-full protest.

'I'm going to scrape you up some carrots,' he says. Shy, daring: 'You're feeding my baby that crap.'

Sita makes a face, a Sita-face. 'Oh, your baby,' she says. 'Our baby. Everyone's baby. Possibly and additionally Salm's baby, please don't forget.'

Her kitchen is tiled like a lav, floor to ceiling. He knows it well. He rinses her sweet down the sink, cores two apples, slices them onto a plate. Back to the bedroom.

It's the old story, a silly old story, this love and babies. What kind of combination is that, anyway? Martin thinks. He lies down beside her, touches her belly, waits for her to flinch, realizes – as she doesn't – she won't. That's the other one, who maybe loves him and pushes him around. Who won't relax without a fight. Gently, he strokes.

'She's the lady of leisure, these days,' Sita is saying.

'She's insane,' Martin responds, closing his eyes. Sleep is stealing warmly up his back, around his head. It's three in the afternoon, but his body is still clocked to Italy.

* * *

Usually he leaves at dusk, the moon pale as a clock. This time, his error – past ten. The pillows smelling of maple syrup.

Oh, these women, thinks Martin, as Sita shifts in his arms, in her sleep. These smart women everywhere. And now trouble's banner is up. You betray this person by making that person, you mess with the wrong molecular slush. One day they could meet, even, Hero and the bad baby, but not yet, not today, don't fall back to sleep, Martin tells himself, think of a reason, dress so quickly....

Getting to know each other:

'I'm depressed,' Claudia says.

'You're not depressed, you're bored. Depressed is for big girls.'

Hero has the stereo gunning – Miles Davis, *Concierto de Aranjuez*. Claudia is reading *Oedipus at Colonus*. The whole week past has rained dirt. Now they're in a thunderous hour – vague top notes relieved by the bass kick, the thing itself.

Claudia throws *Oedipus* at the black sky beyond plate glass. It bounds off. 'Can I play with your make-up?'

'If I had any …'

'Wine? Cigarettes? Hairspray?'

They listen together to something in the music, the same cool little catch, until it falls away. Hero stretches her long self. 'Tomorrow we'll buy guitars and lipstick.'

'You bore the piss out of me,' Claudia says. Hero smiles. 'And where's Martin?'

'Having supper at a fancy restaurant with a nice lady friend of ours who needs some legal advice, and he won't be back until after your bedtime, which is imminent.'

'Couple of big assumptions there.'

'Five, by my count. Juice?'

Claudia shakes her head. 'You're gonna distract me with juice? I think not.'

And – gone.

And Hero, the little lump, alone in the big house, blanket-swathed, just listening, just letting her music mark his time.

* * *

The day she left, a Friday, the firm bought her lunch at the crêpe restaurant. They thought she was sick.

'This looks nourishing,' said a secretary, pointing to an item on the menu. 'A colourful medley of Provençal vegetables with a gay sprinkling of fresh herbs.'

'No, look at her colour, she needs protein,' said a senior partner. They started to squabble. The secretary, displeased, checked the clasp on every piece of jewellery she wore – earrings, necklace, bracelets. She scrunched her hair, groomed her eyebrows, touched her little finger to the corner of her mouth to check for lipstick. She was a handsome, speckless woman in her sixties.

'You're a mess, aren't you?' Lee, another partner, asked. Lee was a friend.

'Everyone is so wrong, but me,' she said.

* * *

Here are two things she does now: running and playing. They fill her days, like breathing in and breathing out.

Running is pure rhythm, and a long self-feeding pain. At the end of an hour's run she will speed up, pulling the sprint out like a magic card – then ease, gasp and retch. But her legs grow shapes and pads of muscle. She can breathe and breathe.

* * *

Martin twists a beer from its plastic choker, cracks it. Hero is on her back, on the carpet, talking about Bach. Her belly is flat, her skin pure, her hair shiny and new, clipped like a swimmer's. She goes running every day, deep sleeps on the sofa in front of the TV. He knows she has packed books and tapes into her car. Probably cash too, jeans and tea. She is laying a good stone foundation, for something.

'... crusades. Medieval music is scary. And that scariness I hear in Bach. You have to *keep up*, right? It's relentless. It says, "You can't stay with me? Fine. I'm going on ahead. You can *try* to catch up. You can *run*. You probably won't make it, so what?" It's like, you learn the notes, you learn the speeds, you learn the voices, you learn to *touch*, you have it all in place, and you're still on the outside. You're still knocking on this door, going, "Hello?"'

'Remember me?'

'Exactly.'

It's always sad to hear bright people get passionate, Martin thinks. They never sound quite as bright.

'Then, when you get it, when you finally get it, **you** realize you were never important anyway. And as soon as you realize *that*, you

142

lose the thing in the music. Like it's saying, "Ha! Are you listening?"'

No, he isn't, not really. More and more, he just needs to think about Sita. This time a memory, an easy one – before their families came to know, before anyone, even they, knew – their sophomore date, when each determined, over the course of a delicate evening – movie, Chinese, more movie, drive – that the other was not unstable or physically dangerous, and it was all right to be alone together.

Sita, in those days, drove a dainty little navy Corolla. She had a basement suite in a trillionaire's house, across the road from the beach. Taking his hand, she led him through the front garden and around the side of the house, past white roses and toffee-coloured slugs. It was a summer dawn – light, hot, damp and tender. Her door was bolted extravagantly.

The living area was dim and low, with a motel unit kitchenette and a desk she had painted a high-gloss sapphire enamel, black to his eyes, sunstruck, weakened. Here they removed their shoes, and she poured them each a glass of water.

The bedroom, in contrast, had a high white ceiling. It was a relief to enter. A door off the bedroom yielded all the good smells of a clean bathroom. They took turns.

He will remember this: her black stockings, draped over a painted chair, held the bow curves of her calves and feet.

Finally he turned her away from him, and held her. They lay twinned, like an old couple, or brushstrokes on a white page.

* * *

'But after Bach dies, this thing in the music disappears. I mean, in Christendom, it's *gone*. Spain had it. Islam has it. France? Germany? America? Forget it. Two hundred years of sugar.'

'Opera,' Martin protests.

She closes her eyes.

'Sita's pregnant,' he says.

'I know.'

* * *

With Hero, much later, he will feel younger. She is more nearly his equal in height and strength, and when she undresses herself – as she insists on doing – her T-shirt, her socks, could be his. Mornings she is dozy and depressed, eyes squinched against the light, staggering a little, as though sleep were a fight she had lost.

VI

The second time, while Martin was in Italy:

There are four listings of 'Flannery, K.' in the phone book.

'Hi, you've reached Kim, Michael and Paws. We can't come to the phone right now, although Paws will probably be barking at you while you leave your message. He just hates the machine, not like some people we know, he's such a technophobe for a Shelty –'

'Die off,' Hero said, hanging up.

Number two yielded a broguey baritone. 'May I speak to Kathleen Flannery?'

A slight pause. 'Me ma's dead.'

'Jesus.'

'Yeah.'

'Sorry.'

'Ah, I'm over it. Forty-three years, you get over it.'

Hero propped temple on fingertips, squinting. 'Kathleen Flannery, the pianist?'

The voice barked mirth. 'Not bloody likely. More like Kathleen Flannery, the ladies' washroom attendant at Boyle's.'

A woman's voice came on an extension. 'Kieran, will you hang the fuck up. I want to make a call.'

'Sorry,' Hero whispered, placing the receiver gently, gently in its cradle.

* * *

Number three was the one, almost.

* * *

So now this girl, this niece, was leading her up six flights in a murky midday indoor darkness. On the second floor Hero found a light switch and twitted it up and down a few times. It gave a hollow click. The girl waited patiently.

At a door, she hesitated. 'I think she'll disappoint you.'

The old woman sat by a window, manuscripts in her lap. The girl whispered something into her ear and was dismissed from the room by a hand grossly distended: knuckles red and swollen, fingers unnaturally long, as though each digit had been plucked from its socket, left useless and dangling.

She turned to look at Hero. Old age had torn into her face. She did not see. 'Would you like my autograph?' she asked.

Hero took a pencil from the piano and offered it to her along with a scrap of staff paper. The woman couldn't hold the pencil. It slipped to the floor as her fingers worked to grasp it.

'I hope you've not come for a lesson,' she said. 'I no longer teach. Also the piano needs tuning. I tell her but she won't see to it. She says it was tuned last month but it's a lie. She lies and steals from me. They'd be shocked if they knew.'

'Flannery?'

'My peers.'

'It's Hero, Flannery.'

'A good piano is like a crisp green apple,' she said.

Hero cleared her throat.

'But you're no pianist.'

'No, ma'am.'

'What are you?'

'Just – lawyer, ma'am.'

'Ah, well, in that case,' she said. 'My niece will show you out. Magdalena?'

Back in the hall, the girl said, 'Maggie, please. Honestly, *Magdalena*, the holy whore. It's embarrassing, you know?'

'I didn't know. About your aunt,' Hero said.

'Don't worry. She doesn't either.'

At the door, this Maggie slapped her denimed hips. 'See these? I bought them at a celebrity charity auction. These jeans once belonged to Faye Dunaway, the film actress.'

'My,' said Hero, crying now.

'Fit me *exactly*,' said the girl.

VII

Martin's house was a child of the sixties and a famous, furious, draft-dodging American architect. Its blueprints are notorious for their complexity and bumble-bee physics. The structure itself, thanks to foliage and angles, can no longer be photographed adequately for reproduction in spiff coffee table retrospectives of the architect's work, although a single photograph, shot from a helicopter swaying out over the ocean one fine summer's day in 1970, before the pines had grown up, hangs in the private collection of the architect's widow.

One of the house's many daft design features is a hand-cranked retractable roof, to let furniture in, or out. Hero and Martin have just seen the piano winched up into the trees by a crane, a process of hours. It hangs there while the movers eat lunch. Their trucks block the gravel driveway, so that when Sita arrives she must drive around them, onto the grass verge.

'I won't make any sword-of-Damocles jokes if you won't,' Martin says. They stand with their backs to the precipice, elbows on the iron railing, at ease. Sita doesn't get out of her car.

Hero looks straight up, for the first and last time. You'd think it would swing a little, rotate like a pendulum, but it's too heavy; or the world, again, this morning, too still.

'When is it you're leaving?' she asks.

* * *

Salm in his Armani suit, Hero in Guerlain: the cuckolds at lunch.

'I'll make you eat,' Salm says. Pan-Pan at noon glitters and clinks. He recites the menu. Scooped shadows are grained into the soft flesh beneath his eyes. 'But no lemon, no arugula, no beer for you,' he says. 'We forget that the mind is also a body part.'

'This is so nice of you, lunch,' Hero says. 'We could have gone somewhere else.'

'No,' he says. 'No, because I want you to try my new peach soup and tell me what you think.'

She notices the kids he hires as cooks and waitresses are solicitous. They often touch him – a hand on his shoulder in passing, as they go to attend other tables, or crouched beside him to receive subtle instruction. A tall girl in a smock and glasses straightens his perfect tie, dusts his immaculate shoulders with her fingertips. Sita has been gone a week.

'Here is my big plan,' Salm says. 'Coloured meals. You order the yellow special, you get corn, champagne, I don't know, custard. Green, obviously, salad, chartreuse, grapes, honeydew melon. Blue is harder, berries, ok. Maybe just a blue sweet. Black, you know, we burn this, burn that, drink Guinness.'

Hero laughs. 'Gimmick.'

'Principle! Fast food chains have used it for ages. Meat, bun, chicken, gravy, fries, salad, hot dog, fudge sauce, all brown. Look at their success.' They sit back as one of Salm's teenagers places their pretty, mint-sprigged soups. He gives her a wink and a thumbs-up and she retreats, smiling.

'White,' Hero offers quietly. 'Cake, rice.'

'I hope their plane goes down.'

* * *

(Claudia has been away. India? College? She is independent now, wilful as her mother, coming and going as she pleases. But here are her parents at the airport, come to fetch her home.

'Have you seen my passport?' Sita says, pressing a fist into the small of her back. 'Possibly I left it in the washroom. Never mind, I have to go back anyway.'

'Wow, again,' Martin says, smiling.

'I'm pregnant.'

'I know it.'

Waiting, he watches times on the Arrivals board, numbers turning over like odds at a track. Seven weeks to go. She will be brown-skinned. When they bring her home, a blue hospital band to clip from her tiny wrist. She will get so angry, little fists and kicking. When she gets older they will argue so he can say tasty things like, Fuck off back to Yale.

147

The airport is like a mall with a purpose, a starfish barnacled with shops, its arms routes to everywhere. Martin stands in the hub, with its great glass-domed ceiling, approving of the currents of activity all around. His shoulders are strung with luggage, his and Sita's. He is the traveller, now.

He buys a coffee, to connect himself to the swirl and business around him. His contentment is utter, although he hasn't seen Claudia in weeks. Her ghost, her husk, fell away.

But then they call his flight; and see, she is walking towards him, the one in the world, slowly, crossing the starfish, passport in hand. Here she comes.)

* * *

I should hurt more, Hero thinks.

'Then you interested me, for a while. And I thought, why not? Why shouldn't I?'

Salm is in full confessional mode, miserable, indiscreet. Hero just wants to relax and chew. He has ordered them foil-baked potatoes, the old campfire standby, but stuffed with chicken *korma* and garnished with yoghurt, figs, and almonds. One of Sita's innovations, he says, except Hero has had it before, when Martin served it to her for her birthday last year, or the year before.

'You're a bit dense, though,' Salm says.

Really.

'And this piano business.'

Hero takes another bite of her clever potato. She drinks her water. Salm bangs his fist on the table. 'Don't smile at me!'

* * *

It would have been as difficult for Hero, at thirteen, to perform Bach correctly as to perform a strip-tease correctly. Some girls, Flannery used to say, must *learn*. She has never heard Flannery play. By the time Hero was put in a dress and taken for her audition with the famous lady, the Parkinson's had already been diagnosed, and she taught, shivering, from a chair across the room.

Flannery this, Flannery that. She had had a concert career, yes – oh, with its flotsam of ads, programs, the promotional photo in the waiting room. Every week Hero hated this photo a little more. It showed a young, glamorous, black-and-white Flannery, hands clasped by her cheek, all Irish about the lips and black-eyed and safe, before the wretched palsy, the bitterness, the work with children.

There is a single recording. Flannery mentioned it once. Hero has suckers out – to New York, to London – searching.

Martin was at the last concert Flannery ever gave. He said her runs went up like fountains and came down like rain. He said her chords were beds of thyme. He made Hero a gift of the program. He was just a boy, and his father had taken him to see. Already limping, but she played like a devil. She was angry – Martin's father had explained, Martin explained to Hero, Hero remembered – and that helped.

So: Hero has never heard Flannery. Martin has never heard Hero. Sita has never been to the opera. What to do?

* * *

'It's a long way to go, for an opera.'

'For anything.'

'When are they leaving, again? Sita told me but I didn't take it in.'

* * *

'Thursday,' Martin says.

One of the movers stands, draining a wax quart carton of chocolate milk. He squints up at the piano and back at Hero, smiling. She smiles, too. They are children, delighted with the cartoon they have arranged here, and the additional knowledge that if he released the piano now its plunging weight might shear the famous house right off the face of the cliff, like a too, too prominent nose.

Next to the elevator stands a steel pole the height of a three-year-old. Perched on top is a box with a keypad, a speaker grille, and a hinged glass window the size of a playing card. Its twin, mounted by the kitchen telephone, lacks only this spray of sap-stuck dead pine needles across its face.

As the truck with the crane resumes its grinding and the

movers reach up for the piano's ankles, Hero pops open the window with her fist, picks out the card that says 'Slater/Saarinen', and crumples it.

'May I keep that?' Martin asks.

VIII

This place belonged to Rome. Sita can see it in the stonework planted beneath her feet, in the arcades, in the age-old boredom of the melon vendors. She sees it everywhere, in the arrogant lines of the place and the faces set like coins. Men in aprons, girls fat and gorgeous to slaughter – too fat, anywhere but here.

Heat lies on the city like a hand. The baby inside her kicks and plays. Their hotel is odd and unclean, stifling after dark, but they've stopped having sex and that helps.

'Supper was good.' They lie in separate beds, too far to take hands – thank *God*, she thinks, the silliness, this *heat* – and say things.

'We want stamps.'

'We liked those saints, didn't we?'

'Tomorrow, shoes.'

'Yes.'

'Are you very tired now?' he asks.

Sleep, too, is a city: Venice. She spends nights on dark waters, navigating its domes and rot.

* * *

Oh, possibly she has made a mistake.

They breakfast on dry rolls with margarine, and jam in little plastic matchboxes. The coffee is chicory, grey and smoky. Even the water is carbonated. Now Salm, she thinks, would just give up and die. Herself, she spoons the little jams straight to her tongue. Lately she can taste nothing but sweetness. Martin loves this about her but she worries for the child, little sugar-baby, and for her own teeth. Still, she has trouble downing what she cannot taste.

The weight she can always lose after the child is born. She can run, like Hero. Jog off the slob.

Martin takes it all and pretends to love it – the cheap food, the bad coffee. She decides he must be superstitious.

After breakfast, back in their room before leaving for the day, he likes to cream her up with sunblock. Face, hands – any excuse to touch. She hates it. 'I don't burn,' she snaps. He makes her sit and kneels at her feet, easing off her sandals. She grips the arms of the chair and stares straight ahead while he works on her feet, smearing.

She's a princess, no doubt about it. Later, in the market, he buys her a sandalwood fan, which she wears dangling from her wrist.

She's not oblivious to irony. She watched that day from her car as Hero stripped the name-card from the intercom, made a fist of it, and palmed it to Martin, who smoothed it to fit in his wallet like a business card. It's still there – Sita checks every dawn. Opera, opera, opera, she thinks.

But Hero shouldn't be here, and she is, and she's having a marvellous time. She buys a lot of good linen clothes and drinks like a pirate with every meal. Sita can't blink her back. She strides around corners in her loose, cool dresses. She gets everywhere first, the silver trails of her fingertips like slug-lines along the walls. *You never came!* Sita protests. *This isn't yours!*

The baby is Salm's, she is pretty sure.

* * *

The opera lives in the dark heart of the city, the arena. All roads ray toward it. Sita imagines Romans leading lions through these streets, and slaves in swinging iron cages. She thinks she needs endings, in this penultimate month, the way other women are supposed to need pickles.

Outside the arena, they are obliged to queue for two hours in the brassy swelter of a foreign afternoon. She sits heavily on Martin's sweater and obliges with the fan, which seems less of a gift when she realizes he has always had this place in mind. Finally, a policeman comes from within to open the gates outwards, and the crowd tenses and surges. The iron gate catches Martin's shoulder and stops in its ponderous swing. A wave of voices mounts from behind as their bodies press him forward. A woman screams tumbling abuse into his face and he frowns as neither the gate nor his shoulder seems inclined to yield. Later that night he will be disappointed to discover the bruising he feels is not more evident. They will frown over it together. His shoulder's flesh is soft and white, like fruit grown in a cave, and will barely discolour. But now he clings to her hand as to a thread through a labyrinth as they are finally brushed, motes in the amazing crowd, through the gate and into the arena.

★ ★ ★

(This is a dream. This is the dream of a girl for whom nothing is yet real.)

ACKNOWLEDGEMENTS

'Black', 'Letters and Numbers' and 'Awake' were first published in *The Malahat Review*; 'Sexy Rex' in *Event*; 'Stars' and 'Things' in *The New Quarterly*; 'Run' in *TickleAce*; 'Trials' in *Grain*; 'Joe in the Afterlife' in *Border Crossings*; and 'Hounds' and 'Watch Me' in *Fiddlehead*. 'Hounds' was also reprinted in the Turnstone Press anthology *Fresh Blood: New Canadian Gothic Fiction*.

Thanks to Caroline Adderson, Zsuzsi Gartner and Rick Loughran for their time and energy. Above all, I am grateful to Linda Svendsen and John Metcalf for their unfailing patience, enthusiasm, and encouragement.

Annabel Lyon has a degree in philosophy from Simon Fraser University and an MFA in creative writing from the University of British Columbia, where she was fiction editor of PRISM *international*. She currently lives in Vancouver.